Copyright © 2025 by Holly Symons
All rights reserved.

No part of this book may be reproduced, scanned, or distributed in any printed or electronic form without permission.
This book is a work of fiction. Names, characters, places, and incidents are either the product of the author's imagination or used fictitiously.
Hardback - ISBN: 978-1-923567-09-2
Paperback - ISBN: 978-1-923567-10-8
eBook - ISBN: 978-1-923567-11-5

Cover design by **Holly Symons**
First Edition

For More, Please Visit

HollySymons.com.au

The RealmsVerse
Of Mirrors

The Realm That Forgot Her

Chapter One: The Goddess in Her Place

She didn't remember stepping forward, only the feeling of falling.

One breath, she was in the Mirror of the Realms, watching Arexia walk through it like a queen reclaiming a crown she'd never earned. The next?

Light.

Blinding, pearlescent, too perfect to be real.

Medusa opened her eyes slowly. The floor beneath her was marble, so clean it reflected her face in a thousand tiny slivers. But... not quite her face. Her serpents were still. Her dress shimmered in gold. Her skin, glowing like moonlight dusted in glitter.

She didn't wear this.

She wouldn't wear this.

"Your Majesty," a voice purred from the shadows. "You're awake."

Medusa jerked upright. Pain didn't follow. Odd. She was never not sore after a mirror-crossing. A woman approached, cloaked in white with an obsidian mask covering her eyes. She bowed low.

"It is my honour to welcome you back. The Realm awaits. We've prepared your favourites: roasted phoenix eggs, blood peach nectar, and one of the remaining hydra hearts. Seared, just how you like it."

"I don't like any of those," Medusa said flatly.

The woman smiled. "Of course not. Not yet."

Two massive golden doors opened at the far end of the hall with a slow, operatic groan.

Beyond them: a throne room that should have been familiar. But the banners were new. The walls curved in impossible symmetry. And seated around the polished crystal banquet table...

Were the gods.

Hera in shimmering lilac, sipping wine without complaint.
Ares standing at her side, armour polished, expression unreadable.
Even Zeus, lounging on a floating chaise like a bored game show host.

Every one of them turned to her and smiled.

"Our Queen returns," Hera said, lifting her glass.

"Took you long enough," Zeus muttered. "We had bets."

"I lost two horns of ale," Ares said, bowing deeply. "But you're worth it."

Medusa's eyes narrowed. "Why are you all being" she glanced at Hera, "civil?"

Zeus laughed. "Because you fixed everything, sweetheart. No more rebellion. No more war. No more serpents chewing on the dinner guests. You're the queen we always hoped you'd be."

Medusa's serpents twitched. Or tried to.

They didn't move.

She lifted a hand to her head. They weren't there.

Bound. Silenced.

Golden rings held each serpent tightly against her scalp like a jewelled crown. They weren't hissing. They weren't alive.

They weren't hers.

"What did you do to me?" she whispered.

From across the room, a mirror flickered.

And in it… she moved.

Only it wasn't her.

Not quite.

The woman in the mirror raised a hand a moment too late. Her smile was wider. Her gown darker. Her eyes… satisfied.

"Welcome home," the reflection said. "Let's see how long you last this time."

Chapter Two: Zeus Throws a Couch

It started with a couch.

More specifically, it started with Zeus throwing a couch at Odin's head.

Medusa didn't blink. She just stood at the edge of the throne room, trying to decide if this was some sort of godly mating ritual or a hallucination caused by too much phoenix egg vapour.

"You tried to touch my thunderbolt," Zeus growled, lobbing the golden chaise like a discus.

"I thought it was a door handle!" Odin snapped back, ducking as the couch exploded against a pillar. "Your kingdom is built like a drunk roc designed it with a glue stick!"

"Why is he here?" Hera hissed, dramatically shielding her goblet of wine like it might be poisoned by Norse incompetence.

"I don't know," Medusa muttered. "I went through the mirror, not a mythology blender."

The scene devolved quickly.

Ares joined in not to defend anyone, but because Zeus had thrown something and he hadn't yet. He picked up a marble statue of Aphrodite (head already missing, suspicious) and hurled it at the ceiling. It bounced.

"WAR!" Ares roared, not helping.

Hera clapped her hands once, summoning a divine barrier around her wine glass. Then she sat down and started updating her to-smite list.

"Don't you people have a mirror goddess to worship or something?" Odin muttered.

Medusa inhaled slowly. "You mean me?"

Odin stared at her, confused. "No. The one with the glowing eyes and permanent resting judgment face. She said to wait here until she returned from... something. Scrubbing a prophecy? No spa day. That was it. She was going to fix her aura in a mineral spring."

"Arexia," Medusa whispered.

Of course she was already three steps ahead. And she'd left them here with each other.

"She left you in charge?" Hera snorted. "Well. That explains the mood."

"What mood?" Medusa asked.

The ground rumbled.

The chandelier above flickered.

And behind the throne, the mirror cracked.

Just a little.

"That one," Hera said. "The apocalyptic one."

"We're in a trap," Medusa said softly. "And the only way out is to find the woman wearing my face."

Interlude: The Mani-Pedis of Destiny

Arexia hummed to herself as a celestial attendant soaked her fingers in molten starlight.

"More glitter," she said, not looking up.

The attendant, an underpaid sylph with too many eyes, nodded nervously and summoned a tray of diamond-dusted soul lacquer.

Next to her, Aurelya was trying to read a prophecy scroll while a salamander massaged her calves with volcanic oil.

"This feels illegal," Aurelya muttered, squinting. "And slightly prophetic."

"Everything I do is technically prophetic," Arexia said sweetly. "It's not my fault the

Realms underestimated the healing power of exfoliation."

Whifflina, one of the whiffles is their assigned Realm Concierge, sat in a lotus pose near the edge of the spa pool. She was meditating, or trying to.

"I regret everything," she whispered into his paws.

Sir Sparkles was nearby, in a kimono that said 'Queen Energy Only' across the back. He was drinking a Realm-Tini and watching two mermaids fight over an enchanted loofah.

"This is why I don't leave the lounge dimension," he said flatly. "One goddess steals a crown and suddenly the spa's booked for eternity."

Aurelya leaned over toward Arexia.

"So, be honest. What's actually going on in Olympus?"

Arexia smiled wide, relaxed, dangerous.

"Oh, they're fighting. Probably over nothing. Or over something I said before leaving. I may have implied Zeus's thunderbolt was compensating."

"For what?"

"Exactly."

She sipped her drink, which sparkled violently.

"You know what I love about traps?" she added.

Aurelya raised an eyebrow. "No, but I'm assuming you're about to tell me."

"Watching everyone thinks they're clever enough to escape one I haven't even finished designing."

A mirror on the wall flickered. It showed Zeus throwing a chaise. Ares shouting "WAR!" Hera summoning a wine shield. Odin getting hit with something heavy.

Arexia chuckled.

"And they haven't even met the minotaur with trust issues yet."

Aurelya rolled her eyes and sipped her drink.

"You're the villain, aren't you?"

"Darling," Arexia said, flipping her perfectly lacquered nails toward the mirror. "I'm the rewrite."

Chapter Three: The Mirror Is a Liar

Loki arrived late.

Fashionably, obviously.

He stepped through the cracked hallway, trailing chaos sparkles, holding what appeared to be a flaming scroll, half a croissant, and a boot he definitely stole from Odin.

"Did I miss breakfast or just the mandatory emotional breakdown?"

Zeus groaned. "Why is he here?"

"Because your version of Olympus runs on passive-aggressive denial and I thrive in that ecosystem," Loki replied, tossing the croissant at Ares, who caught it and tried to bite it, only to find it was made of wax.

Medusa had her arms crossed, eyes locked on the cracked mirror behind the throne. It shimmered. It pulsed. It whispered things only she could hear.

"It's lying," she said. "It keeps showing me what I want to see."

Loki moved beside her, unusually serious.

"That's what this Realm does. It gives you the life you think you earned... until you forget what you were trying to fix in the first place."

"How do you know that?" Medusa asked.

He grinned. "Because I invented it. Sort of. It was a prank."

Everyone stared.

"You pranked an entire Realm?" Hera asked.

"Technically, I just misplaced a prophecy and rewired a pocket dimension during a bet with a unicorn bard. It's all very complicated."

Odin muttered, "This is why no one invites you to apocalypse planning meetings."

The mirror pulsed harder. This time, it showed Arexia smiling in a hot spring with Aurelya and drinking from a skull-shaped coconut.

"She knows we're watching," Medusa said.

"Of course she does," Loki said. "She's me, but with better skincare and worse morals."

The mirror began to ripple more violently now, glitching.

Suddenly, a message scrawled itself across the glass in shimmering golden flame:

"IF YOU WANT TO FIND ME, YOU HAVE TO WIN MY GAME."

And below that: a symbol none of them recognised.

Except Loki.

He went pale.

"Oh no," he whispered. "Not that Realm. That Realm has… singing skeletons. And a Minotaur with abandonment issues."

Zeus folded his arms. "What kind of game are we talking?"

Loki sighed.

"The kind where we need a bard, a weapon forged in embarrassment, and someone brave enough to ride a rabid manticore named Glitterfang."

Ares perked up. "I call the manticore."

"This isn't just a trap," Medusa said. "It's a rewritten story. And she's making us play by her plot."

Chapter Four: The Bard with a Bone Xylophone

Ares didn't like walking.

He especially didn't like walking through glittery forest paths that sparkled every time he swore.

"I said war, not whimsy," he growled, kicking a flower that chirped "No thank you!" in response.

"You're hurting the terrain's feelings," Loki called back. "Try being less emotionally volatile, thunder thighs."

"You have thigh envy," Ares muttered.

They'd entered the first trial Realm in Arexia's twisted breadcrumb trail a pastel-glitched forest called The Echoed Vale, where everything echoed back at you in compliments or insults. It was exhausting.

Medusa stayed quiet. Hera summoned a mosquito net made of divine silk. Zeus had summoned a lounge chair with wheels and was having Whiffles push him.

Then came the singing.

Bones clacked in rhythm. A deep bass beat vibrated from somewhere near a moss-covered log. The grass started dancing.

Ares raised a brow. "Is that a skeleton with… bongos?"

It was.

And not just any skeleton.

A glitter-dusted bard with sunglasses, a rainbow scarf, and a full bone xylophone strung across his ribs.

"WELCOOOOOME TO THE VALE!" he sang in a baritone that made butterflies faint. "I'M YOUR GUIDE, YOUR VIBE, YOUR NEON-TONED TRIBE AND I'LL ONLY HELP YOU... IF YOU RAP FOR YOUR LIFE!"

"No," Hera said immediately.

"Yes," Loki said, too fast.

Ares scowled. "We don't have time for this. I'm a god of war. Not... rhythm."

"Then you die in rhyme," the bard sang, snapping his femurs like drumsticks.

Medusa looked at Ares, lips twitching.

"Come on. You took down hydras. You can handle a rap battle."

Ares groaned.

He stepped forward, cracked his knuckles, and sighed. "Fine."

"Yo, I'm Ares, the god of brawls and bruises,

I fight with fists, not clever muses.

If you want rhythm, go ask the Fates

I only rhyme when I annihilate!"

The bard paused... then slowly nodded.

"That... was terrible. But emotionally honest. You pass."

The mirror behind the bard shimmered and opened. A sigil glowed above it.

Loki leaned over to Ares and whispered, "You actually rhymed 'Fates' and 'annihilate.' That was horrifyingly impressive."

"Shut up," Ares grumbled, walking through the portal.

"One Realm down," Medusa said, watching the mirror close behind them. "Only several ridiculous ones to go."

Interlude: Two Chapters Behind and Dressed for the Wrong Plot

Dionysus was late.

Again.

Technically, he arrived on time but to the wrong timeline. He stumbled through a mirror, juggling a golden goblet, three confused nymphs, and what might have been a portable disco ball blessed by Apollo.

"IS THIS THE KARAOKE REALM?!" he yelled into the void.

It was not.

It was a swamp. Filled with angry frogs. One threw a shoe at him.

Dionysus blinked, adjusted his laurel crown (sideways), and sipped from his goblet.

"Note to self: This is not Chapter Five."

He stumbled onward, dragging a glitter-coated luggage bag that squeaked with every wheel rotation. Inside: seventeen wigs, one emergency toga, and an unopened letter labelled "Catch Up Already Love, Hades."

Somewhere, far ahead, the others were fighting cursed bards or climbing screaming staircases. But Dionysus? He was getting heckled by moss.

"Stop narrating at me!" he shouted at a particularly judgmental tree.
The tree did not stop.

Eventually, he found a map. It was upside down. Also, possibly a pizza menu. But he declared it helpful and used it as a cape.

"I'm coming, Medusa!" he declared to a bewildered squirrel.

"No, I'm not late. You're all just early."

He tripped on a vine. Again.

And from the distance, you could hear it: the chaotic mutterings of a drunken god, echoing into the Realms.

"Wait... are we on Chapter Four or Chapter Six?!"

Chapter Five: Glitterfang Rides Again

Hera refused to enter a stable that smelled like singed fur and broken dreams.

"This is beneath me," she said, clutching a perfumed handkerchief over her nose.

"It's not beneath you," Loki said. "It's beside you. And it's trying to lick your shoe."

Glitterfang, the manticore in question, stood ten feet tall and shimmered in every direction at once. His mane sparkled like a unicorn lost a bet to a disco ball. His tail was part-scorpion, part-firework, and fully offended by silence.

He roared.

Not a terrifying, beastly roar.

A fabulous, overacted one.

"RAAAHHHhrrawwwrr-uhhh," he drawled, tossing his head. "Someone announce me properly, or I bite something."

Whiffles, holding a clipboard that said Magical Beasts & Disappointments, cleared his throat.

"Glitterfang the Magnificent, fourth of his name, undefeated in mirror-beast racing, retired champion of the Frosthorn Games, and probable traitor."

"I heard that," Glitterfang said, sulking. "I was framed."

Ares stepped forward, eyes gleaming. "I want to ride him."

Glitterfang snorted. "No offence, big guy, but I don't carry insecure energy. Try therapy first."

"You're insulting a god," Ares growled.

"I'm elevating a conversation," Glitterfang purred.

Hera turned to Medusa. "Why is he like this?"

"Because Arexia made him," Medusa said, narrowing her eyes.

That made everyone pause.

Glitterfang, noticing the shift in tone, flicked his tail and looked too casual.

"I'm not saying I'm spying on you. I'm just saying I see everything. Through time. And mirrors. And spa water."

Loki grinned. "That's either terrifying or very on-brand for this quest."

Zeus sighed from the hay bale throne he'd conjured. "We need the glitter cat to open the next Realm, don't we?"

"Yes," Medusa said. "But only if he lets us ride him through the Rift Path."

Everyone turned back to Glitterfang.

He smiled. Bright. Sharp.

"Beg," he said.

Ares cracked his knuckles.

Medusa summoned her glare.

Hera... took one step forward, adjusted her crown, and said in the most regal voice known to divinity:

"Pretty please."

Glitterfang gasped.

"Well. That's new."

He lowered himself with exaggerated flair. "Get on, darlings. Let's ride."

"I'm riding a rainbow disaster with a scorpion tail," Hera muttered. "This quest is cursed."

Chapter Six: The Realm of Screaming Statues

The second Realm smelled like limestone and regret.

The trees were carved marble. The grass was polished granite. And the air vibrated with the sound of soft, constant whispering.

Whiffles checked the mirror gate behind them. It sealed shut with a pop and a glittery sigh.

"Well, we're locked in. Again. That's normal. That's fine. That's good for the nerves."

"Why are the statues looking at me?" Zeus asked, nervously adjusting his lightning-buckle.

"Because" Medusa said slowly, "they're alive."

As if on cue, one of the nearest statues a hunched gargoyle with a suspicious nose ring turned its head and screamed.

"I ONCE SEDUCED A DRAGON FOR A BAG OF COINS AND A SANDWICH!"

Zeus flinched. "Okay, that wasn't me. But it's a strong opener."

The statues screamed again. A cacophony of personal confessions, awkward truths, and divine regrets echoed through the stone trees:

"LOKI KISSED HIMSELF IN ANOTHER TIMELINE!"
"HERA SECRETLY SHIPS HERACLES AND MEDUSA!"
"ARES ONCE CRIED DURING A KITTEN COMMERCIAL!"
"ZEUS THINKS ODIN HAS BETTER ABS!"

Everyone froze.

Ares covered his ears. "Make it stop!"

"YOU CAN'T HIDE FROM WHO YOU ARE!" the statues chanted in unnerving harmony.

Glitterfang, lounging like a judgmental housecat, purred. "Arexia really outdid herself with this Realm. Brutal and well-curated."

Medusa stepped forward. The statues closest to her quieted, then tilted.

"THEY WHISPER ABOUT YOUR CROWN. THEY SAY YOU STOLE IT. THEY SAY YOU WERE NEVER MEANT TO RULE."

She flinched.

"They're wrong," she muttered.

"They're statues," Loki offered. "They scream feelings. I wouldn't take them too seriously unless they start tap dancing."

One of them tap danced.

Medusa sighed. "Of course."

The screaming continued, then suddenly… cut off.

A single statue a large, winged lion opened its mouth and whispered in a voice that echoed with prophecy:

"TO FIND THE SPA DAY QUEENS, FACE YOUR TRUE FORM. FIND THE ONE WHOSE VOICE DOES NOT LIE."

Loki narrowed his eyes. "That's either poetic or a warning about someone's ex."

A path opened in the stone forest, glowing softly beneath their feet.

Medusa exhaled.

"Let's go. Before they scream anything about me and Hades."

"TOO LATE," a statue shrieked.

"This Realm is a trauma dump with better acoustics," Loki said. "And I hate how much I relate."

Interlude: The Rum-Scented Detour of Dionysus

Dionysus had absolutely no idea where he was.

Again.

He swaggered into the Realm of Screaming Statues with all the grace of a half-sober pirate god on a booze cruise detour. His toga was askew, his laurel crown was on backwards, and he was inexplicably riding a shopping trolley made entirely of golden vines.

"Who's in charge here?" he slurred at a statue mid-scream. "Blink once for yes, twice for dramatic flair."

The statue screamed louder.

Unfazed, Dionysus pulled out a half-empty

bottle of ambrosia wine and took a swig. "Don't worry, I speak fluent melodrama."

A gust of magical wind blew his toga up like a scandalous prophecy. He saluted a passing squirrel. "You saw nothing."

Somewhere in the distance, Hercules was battling enchanted armour. Medusa was busy interrogating a screaming bust. But Dionysus?

He was attempting to trade a cursed spoon for directions.

"Look, it glows *and* insults your enemies! It called me a cabbage!"

The spoon glowed ominously and hissed, "He lies."

Dionysus stared. "That's rich coming from a

utensil with rage issues."

Suddenly, a ghostly statue lunged toward him.

He threw the spoon.

The spoon insulted the statue's mother.

They both exploded.

Covered in glitter and statue dust, Dionysus brushed himself off and shouted to no one in particular, "That was a tactical distraction!"

The trolley rolled away on its own, humming a sea shanty.

Dionysus chased it, slipping on statue gravel and shouting, "WAIT! MY WINE!"

And from far above, a single crow muttered,

"He's two chapters behind again."

To which Dionysus replied, "I prefer the term:

narratively delayed!"

Chapter Seven: Whiffles and the Trial of Self-Respect

Whiffles was not built for self-reflection.

He was built for sarcasm, concierge work, and emergency gossip evacuation. Not this.

He stood alone in a glittering maze, every wall made of mirrors. Some showed him in his Realm staff uniform. Others showed… other versions. Taller ones. Confident ones. One of them wore a tiny crown.

He hated that one the most.

"Why do I look like I run a cult in that one?" he muttered.

A voice echoed from the air Arexia's, dripping in spa-day smugness.

"Welcome to your Trial of Self-Respect. You may not leave until you admit you're more than just a commentary sidekick with anxiety issues."

"I reject the premise," Whiffles said flatly.

The mirrors pulsed. One of them showed him being ignored during team meetings. Another showed Glitterfang using his notebook as a coaster.

"I SAID I WAS TAKING NOTES," Whiffles snapped. "I WAS CONTRIBUTING STRATEGICALLY!"

The mirrors blinked.

"Really?" one version of himself said in a judgey tone. "Name one strategic thing you've done this week."

"I gave Medusa a mint when she looked like she was going to cry. THAT COUNTS."

The walls trembled.

A door appeared ahead but it was guarded by a huge, terrifying version of himself wearing battle armour and carrying a flaming ledger.

"YOU SHALL NOT PASS UNTIL YOU SAY SOMETHING NICE ABOUT YOURSELF," it boomed.

Whiffles blinked.

"I once solved a logistics issue between a demigod and a centaur in under ten minutes?"

The floor glowed.

"And I make exceptional tea," he added quickly.

The mirror version stared.

"Also, I have amazing cheek fluff and a sarcastic wit that masks deep abandonment trauma and a very small sense of optimism!"

The mirror cracked and so did the wall.

The maze dissolved, revealing a path to rejoin the others.

Whiffles took a deep breath.

"Okay. Fine. I'm a little bit heroic. One time. Under duress. Never again."

Loki was waiting at the exit, sipping something suspiciously fizzy.

"Well look who passed emotional torture with flying colours."

"I cried on a statue of myself," Whiffles said. "It was a whole thing."

"Arexia's not just testing us," Whiffles muttered. "She's rewriting who we think we are one humiliation at a time."

Chapter Eight: The RealmVision Roadblock

Sir Sparkles was not amused.

He had just finished exfoliating, reheating his drink, and fixing his fourth sequin emergency of the day when RealmVision pulled him back in.

The mirror spat him out mid-air into a blinding neon arena, surrounded by floating platforms, glitter cannons, and a very aggressive disco ball.

"WHY AM I IN GLAM MODE WITHOUT WARNING?" he shouted as he landed in a feathered heap.

A booming voice echoed from all directions. It was Arexia. Again.

"Welcome, contestants, to REALMVISION: SING TO SURVIVE. Each of you will perform. Only one will win. All others… may leave emotionally destabilized and covered in glitter."

Sir Sparkles blinked. "That's… honestly, my Tuesdays."

Backstage, the team arrived.

Zeus stared at the stage and groaned. "Oh no. This is one of those trials, isn't it?"

"Yes," Whiffles whispered. "And Sir Sparkles is already trending."

Loki peeked around the curtain. "Are we expected to sing?"

"Or dance," Sparkles called. "Or suffer."

He was now in full sequined regalia and applying rhinestones to his eyebrows.

Medusa sighed. "Can we just not play the game this time?"

The lights dimmed. A giant mirror stage rose from the centre. The music blared.

Arexia's voice returned:

"Contestant One: Sir Sparkles, performing 'Crown Me Again (You Cowards)'."

Sparkles strutted to centre stage, mic in paw, hair glowing like celestial disco fire.

"This one's for all the queens who were told they sparkle too much," he purred. "And the gods who forgot who crowned them."

He sang.

He slayed.

He mic dropped.

He posed.

The mirror opened behind him with a glitter-blast.

He turned and winked at the team.

"You're welcome. Follow me or stay here and battle Valkyries in karaoke."

Zeus raised a hand. "Can I stay and sing?"

"NO," everyone said.

"The mirror liked his falsetto," Loki muttered. "This Realm's officially lost its mind."

Interlude: The Cursed Karaoke Lounge Incident

It was supposed to be a shortcut.

That's what Dionysus told himself as he stumbled through a swirling portal shaped like a glittering microphone and landed face-first on a sequined stage under a banner that read:

"Welcome to the Realm of Cursed Karaoke!"

The crowd? A collection of mildly haunted suits of armour, one banshee with a feather boa, and a centaur with a suspicious tambourine.

"Next up!" croaked the host a floating goblin in a tuxedo. "The god of revelry, in his two-chapters-late debut: Dionysus!"

A spotlight hit him. The mic sparked.

Dionysus blinked. "Do I *know* this realm?"

The centaur clanged the tambourine ominously.

"I'll take that as a no."

He picked up the mic. It bit him.

"Ow! Alright, you want a performance? YOU GET A PERFORMANCE."

He launched into an off-key rendition of *Bohemian Rhapsody*, complete with interpretive dancing, wine bottle percussion, and a dramatic toga twirl that nearly decapitated the banshee's boa.

The suits of armour clapped. Literally. Their gauntlets fell off.

The tambourine exploded.

A disco ball descended from nowhere and promptly shattered on his head.

"I REGRET NOTHING!" Dionysus howled, blood and glitter mingling on his forehead like divine confetti.

Suddenly, the host yelled, "THE CURSE HAS BEEN ACTIVATED!"

The stage floor opened beneath him.

Dionysus plummeted through the floor, still clutching the mic and belting out the last line: "So you think you can stop me and spit in my eyeeeee!”

And then*thud*.

He landed in a cabbage patch. Again.

“Where am I now?” he asked a frog.

The frog croaked: “Chapter Nine.”

Dionysus sighed. “So close. And yet…”

He stood, adjusted his laurel crown, and tossed the mic aside.

“I’ll find them eventually. But first… another song.”

Chapter Nine: The Valkyrie Karaoke Ambush

The mirror portal dropped them into a hallway lined with glowing signs.

Each read the same words:

"KARAOKE OR DEATH"

"THIS IS YOUR FINAL WARMUP"

"NO ONE ESCAPES THE MIC"

Zeus pointed at a flashing disco skull. "This doesn't scream 'safe passage' to me."

Loki sniffed the air. "Smells like betrayal and hairspray."

Whiffles opened a door. "Maybe we just quietly exit"

Wrong.

Because that's when the Valkyries arrived.

Not elegant warriors of legend. Oh no. These Valkyries wore matching pink jumpsuits, carried axe-shaped microphones, and were already mid-chorus of something that sounded suspiciously like a cursed ABBA remix.

"You can dance, you can die, under moonlight with a cry, watch us scream, watch us scream through it aaaaaaalllll!"

Sir Sparkles dropped to one knee. "I both fear and respect this level of commitment."

One Valkyrie stepped forward. Her name tag read: KRYSTAL DEATHWING, LEAD SOPRANO.

"To proceed," she snarled, "you must BATTLE US... in a SING-OFF."

"I choose death," Medusa said instantly.

"Denied," Krystal replied.

Loki stepped up. "Wait. What are the rules?"

"One verse. One dance move. Full eye contact."

Zeus cracked his knuckles. "I was born for this."

"You were born from chaos and poor decisions," Loki muttered.

Round One: Zeus vs Krystal.
He did air guitar on lightning bolts. She sang so high the walls cracked.
Tie.

Round Two: Loki vs Valkyrie Harmony.
He refused to sing, so just mimed in dramatic flair and somehow won anyway.
Winner: Loki.

Final Round: Medusa vs Valkyrie Rage.

Medusa took the mic.

Paused.

Then growled into it:

"Let me pass before I turn you all to stone mid-high note."

The Valkyries screamed. Fled.

Sir Sparkles clapped. "Five stars. No notes. Deeply moving."

The hallway cracked. The walls shimmered.

And a new portal opened this time to a realm cloaked in mist, and something darker.

"This next realm," Medusa said, brushing glitter off her snakes, "better not sing."

Interlude: Dionysus and the Bouncing Barge of Destiny

Dionysus was sailing.

Well bouncing. On what appeared to be a wine barrel hastily repurposed into a raft, complete with a mast made from a pool noodle and a flag that read: "Party or Perish."

"According to my calculations," he said, consulting a soggy map and a compass made from a teacup and a magnet, "I should be only… twelve leagues behind."

A thundercloud rolled in, cackling.

"Oh, shut up!" Dionysus yelled at the sky. "At least I'm trying!"

He tried to row using an oar that was clearly a

ladle. The wine barrel spun in slow, chaotic circles.

Then a foghorn.

No, wait. A duck.

An enormous duck, glowing faintly with eldritch energy, swam past wearing a monocle and muttering about tax policy.

Dionysus blinked. "This is either divine punishment or an enchanted hangover."

Suddenly, the barrel hit something. Hard.

He tumbled off and landed... on a floating tavern.

Its sign read: "*Ye Olde Floating Mistake*."

Inside, a barmaid handed him a drink before he could even protest.

"You're expected," she said.

"By destiny?" he asked.

She shrugged. "No, the karaoke goblin called ahead. Said you'd be late. Again."

Dionysus sighed and took a sip. "Story of my life."

From inside the tavern, a slow chant began:

"Chug. Chug. Chug."

He smiled. "Maybe just one."

Two hours later, he burst through the back

door on a stolen floating keg, yelling, "I'M ON MY WAY!"

The keg veered violently to the left and smacked into a floating tree.

He groaned from the ground. "What chapter is it now?"

A nearby sprite checked a scroll. "Twelve-and-three-quarters."

Dionysus moaned. "Close enough."

He passed out hugging a cheese platter.

Because even gods need snacks.

Just as Dionysus dramatically clutched the cheese platter and sighed, the illusion shimmered, then **popped**.

Gone was the floating tavern.

Gone was the eldritch duck.

Gone was the wine-barrel barge of destiny.

He was lying in an **empty field**. Alone. Holding... a rock.

The "cheese platter" was actually moss.

A few feet away, the others had paused.

Medusa turned. "Dionysus?"

He blinked at her, still half-wrapped in seaweed. "I... I saved us all. From the tax duck."

Loki tilted his head. "You're in a field, Dionysus. You've been in a field for **four hours**. Arguing with your own sandal."

Dionysus looked down.

The sandal glared back. Probably.

Loki smirked, turning to the others. "Come on, let's leave the Wine Goblet of Delusion to his epic quest of **Field Napping and Footwear Diplomacy**."

Without another word, they walked off.

Dionysus raised his ladle-sceptre to the sky.

"I REGRET NOTHING!"

A goat walked by. Judged him silently.

Chapter Ten: Into the Mist of Missing Timelines

Loki didn't like fog.

It was too vague. Too quiet. Too good at hiding things that remembered your name when you forgot theirs.

The team emerged from the glittery karaoke hallway into a realm that didn't start. It just… continued.

Mist clung to their skin like whispering silk. Trees floated, half-rooted in clouds. The ground wasn't solid; it decided to be under your feet, second by second.

"Where are we?" Zeus asked, stepping cautiously. "It's like a memory that got left on pause."

"Or a timeline someone erased," Loki muttered.

Sir Sparkles pulled out a paw mirror. It refused to reflect anything.

"No glamour here. No sparkle. This is deeply rude."

Whiffles touched a hovering fern. It flickered into the shape of a tiny mouse, then a goblin, then Medusa, then disappeared.

"This place doesn't know who we are," Whiffles whispered.

Medusa narrowed her eyes. "Or… we don't."

They kept walking. That was the rule of strange Realms: don't stop. Don't look too long.

The mist thickened. Shapes swirled. Whispers tickled their ears.

Then they saw it.

A massive mirror, but this one didn't show reflections. It showed versions. Whole scenes. Past choices. Futures that never happened. A Medusa who stayed mortal. A Loki who never turned trickster. A Sparkles, who ran a quiet tea shop.

"What is this?" Medusa asked, staring.

"These are the might-have-beens," Loki said, voice low. "And the monsters that feed on them."

Because now the mist had fangs.

A creature lunged, all half-formed regrets and teeth made of forgotten names.

Medusa slashed. Zeus called lightning. Loki cracked illusion into flame.

The beast dissolved, but the mirror cracked with it.

And a voice behind them whispered: "You broke a rule."

They turned.

A small girl stood in the mist, holding a version of Aurelya's crown.

But her eyes were Arexia's.

"This Realm remembers everything you were and everything I plan for you to become."

Chapter Eleven: The Crowned Might-Have-Been

The child wasn't a child.

She wore Aurelya's crown crooked, too large for her head, but her stare was Arexia's: ancient, patient, and made of quiet ruin.

"I remember every version of you," the child said. "Even the one who begged."

Medusa felt her breath catch. "You're not her."

"No," said the girl. "I'm better. I didn't break."

Loki stepped forward, illusion flickering like defensive feathers. "And you're stalling. What is this place?"

"This is what you left behind," the girl whispered. "Every decision. Every fork in the road. Every moment you failed... lives here."

Behind her, the cracked mirror pulsed. One shard flashed: Medusa kneeling before Olympus, chains around her neck.

Another: Aurelya weeping in a ruined temple.

Another: A future where the gods bowed to Arexia alone.

"Stop it," Medusa hissed.

The child, Arexia, tilted her head. "Why? These are yours."

Whiffles hid behind Sir Sparkles. "She's glitching the Realm again…"

"No," Sparkles said, eyes wide. "She's feeding it. The Realm's choosing her story."

Zeus stepped closer to the child. "Let us through. We've got no quarrel with a walking timeline tantrum."

The girl smiled sweetly and vanished.

The mist collapsed inward.

And in her place, three mirror beasts rose, fused from shards of what could have been. One had Medusa's chained hands. One bore Loki's mask, split in two. The third... wore Sparkles' crown but wept.

"We fight our regrets?" Medusa growled, drawing her blade.

"No," Loki said. "We fight her version of us."

Somewhere, far ahead in the fractured Realm... Arexia laughed. And the crown on her real head burned brighter.

Chapter Twelve: When Regret Bites Back

The mirror beasts didn't roar.

They hissed like truths no one wanted spoken.

Medusa charged the version of herself that wore chains. It moved like a queen shackled by silence, every blow choreographed with pity.

"I gave everything," Medusa spat as she struck. "You think silence would've saved us?"

The beast tilted its head and smiled.

Chains lashed out. Wrapped her arms.

She staggered.

Loki, meanwhile, danced with his doppelgänger, the half-masked regret that moved in circles and lies.

"I'm not that version anymore," he hissed.

"Aren't you?" the mask replied. "You never really stopped tricking people. Not even her."

"Especially her," Loki whispered back, eyes flashing with sorrow.

He shattered the illusion, but not before the mask revealed one last shape:

A young girl with wings. Aurelya?

Or Arexia?

The mask vanished.

Sir Sparkles squared off against the weeping, crown-wearing version of himself.

"I'm fabulous. I sparkle in any timeline," he said.

But the creature only cried harder.

"Why do you cry?" he asked, stepping closer.

The beast lifted its head.

"Because you forgot where the crown came from."

Then it crumbled and left behind a single silver memory coin. Sparkles pocketed it in silence.

Whiffles was hiding in a bush.

Zeus was busy punching mist with thunder.

Medusa screamed and broke her chains just as Loki caught her arm.

"You good?"

"No. But I remember who I am now."

The battlefield stilled.

And at its edge, a new doorway formed.

Not a mirror this time.

A stairway.

Carved into stars.

Leading up.

"We climb?" Medusa asked.

"Or we stay here, trapped in who we were,"
Loki said.

They climbed.

Behind them, the Realm of Regret sealed shut,
but the coin in Sparkles' pocket began to glow.

Interlude: The Mist Was Lying (And So Was That Hydra)

Hades drew his blade from the ribcage of a shrieking fog hydra.

The hydra reassembled itself out of existential dread and lunged again.

"This place is hell," Hades muttered.

"You are hell," Hera snapped, flinging a lightning-glamoured spear through the fog. It struck a twelve-eyed banshee with a mouth full of prophecy snakes. "Now keep up."

Hercules was busy suplexing a nightmare centipede the size of a freight train.

"I don't care if it's made of timelines," he grunted. "It touched my hair."

Meanwhile, the rest of the party, about fifty feet ahead, was admiring a floating fern that smelled like cinnamon buns.

"Did you hear something?" Medusa asked.

"Just Sparkles talking to a butterfly," Loki said.

"It's not a butterfly," Sparkles insisted. "It's a metaphor with wings."

Back in the rearguard, Hera side-kicked a despair chimera into a mist fissure.

"We are saving their lives," she snarled. "Again."

"And no one will thank us," Hades added, decapitating a regret dragon with a flick of divine wrath.

Hercules hurled a regret troll into a glowing memory tree, which burst into interpretive dance fire.

"I miss the Underworld," he grumbled. "At least it didn't try to emotionally manipulate me with fog poetry."

"We can't even see the mirror beasts they're talking about," Hera said, scanning the mist. "Because we're too busy fighting the real Realm monsters."

The fog shifted.

And then

"Oh no," Hades said quietly. "She's back."

A creature emerged. She had seven faces, twelve handbags, and a constant need to comment on your confidence levels.

"IS THAT WHAT YOU'RE WEARING?" she shrieked.

"Run," Hera said.

Chapter Thirteen: Staircase to the Skyrealm of Stolen Songs

The stairs didn't just rise, they sang.

Each step hummed with the echo of a memory that didn't belong to them. Notes of lullabies stolen from dying stars. Choruses sung by realms now lost. Whispers of poems never finished.

Medusa's heel hit one stair and

"Hush now, little fangs, don't cry..."
Her mother's voice. Long dead.
Stolen.

She stumbled.

"This Realm's a thief," Hades muttered, gripping the rail. "It's taking the songs that shaped us."

"Or reminding us what we've already lost," Hercules said, strangely quiet.

Sparkles, however, had paused to dramatically harmonise with the floating notes.

"If this place wants a concert, I SHALL DELIVER."

A glowing harp floated by. Whiffles jumped and clung to it like a baby koala.

"Do not touch the instrumental wildlife," Hera warned, swatting a violin bat away from her ear.

They climbed higher.

And with each step, illusions shimmered.

Ares appeared briefly, standing in front of Medusa. He looked younger, with music woven into his armour.

"You once danced with me," the vision said. "And then you chose war."

"I didn't choose," she whispered. "I survived."

The vision vanished.

Zeus was surrounded by symphonic lightning. Hades began to hum an old Underworld requiem under his breath.

Loki paused mid-step, eyes locked on a floating mirror of melody.

"She's near," he said. "The real Aurelya. I heard her song."

"Or Arexia's wearing her voice," Medusa replied.

At the top of the staircase, a massive silver gate shimmered with bars of music staff and floating keys.

"Welcome," a voice echoed. "To the Skyrealm. To pass, play the truth you've buried."

Sparkles bowed, hands extended.

"Finally. A Realm that understands me."

And far below, one broken note dropped like a secret lost back into the mist.

Chapter Fourteen: The Key of Secrets and Discord

The gate shimmered like a locked symphony.

"Play the truth you've buried," the voice echoed again.

Before anyone could ask for clarification, instruments appeared tailored to each soul.

- Medusa received a lyre made of molten bone and obsidian strings.
- Loki's was a flute of glass and regret.
- Sparkles got a golden triangle with too much drama.
- Hera's harp radiated passive-aggressive judgement.
- Hades got an organ that only played in minor existential crises.
- Whiffles got a kazoo. Of course.

One by one, they stepped forward.

Medusa played first.

Her hands trembled. Each pluck of the strings
pulled a truth she hadn't spoken aloud:

"I was powerful before they punished me."
"I didn't need their love to rise."
"But I wanted it anyway."

A single key lit up on the gate.

Loki followed.

Each breath revealed a sliver of his chaos and
his confession:

"I never lied to her. I only wished I had."
"So, I could protect her from what loving me
costs."

Another key shimmered, dissonant but sincere.

Sparkles.

He tapped the triangle dramatically.

"I have seventeen unresolved internal subplots and zero shame."

Nothing happened.

So, he tried again.

"Fine. I stole my own crown. I didn't wait to be chosen."

A key blinked in.

A pause settled over the group.

Then Zeus cleared his throat.

"I, uh... have a confession," he said, shifting awkwardly as the flute of regret passed by his feet.

Everyone turned.

"This better not be another prophecy-child thing," Hera warned, fingers tightening on her harp.

"No, no. This is more... laundry related."

He scratched the back of his neck.

"You remember that one lavender-pink satin thong that went missing from Mount Olympus laundry rotation?"

Everyone froze.

"Zeus," Medusa said slowly, "what did you do?"

"It was comfortable," he said defensively. "And majestic. And I looked great."

Loki fell over laughing.

"You absolute disaster."

"I kept it for emergencies," Zeus muttered. "And confidence."

Sparkles nodded approvingly. "As one should."

"I *knew* it," Hera snarled. "I thought Hermes took it for a prank. But no. *You*"

The gate dinged like a very confused elevator.

"Well," Hades said, "apparently that counts as truth."

"I feel emotionally attacked," Zeus sniffed.

Hera's harp groaned under her fingers, singing of motherhood, resentment, and the pressure to hold power while pretending it was peace.

"I was always a queen. They just never wanted me to enjoy it."

The gate flickered.

But when Hercules tried, his chords rang wrong.

"I'm not ready to admit what I lost."

A discordant boom. The gate screeched.

And from the cracks…

A beast of broken rhythms, constructed from off-key symphonies and mismatched memory shards, erupted.

"Well done," Zeus muttered. "Now we fight a musical demon."

"I blame the kazoo," Hades said.

"I'm using it as a distraction!" Whiffles squeaked, charging into battle with kazoo buzzing.

The gate of the Skyrealm screamed open not with harmony, but with discord, truth, and a very dramatic triangle solo.

Interlude: Surveillance, Sass, and Sudden Difficulty

Arexia sipped her glitter-infused tea from a cup made of actual stardust and tapped her cosmic mirror.

"Let's see how our brave little questers are doing," she purred, lounging in a throne that was equal parts menace and high fashion.

The mirror shimmered, revealing Loki mid-argument with a squirrel wielding a tambourine.

"I don't care how rhythmically inclined you are," Loki snapped, "you can't open with ABBA at a bard battle!"

A few feet away, Hades dragged a clawed hand down his face. "If one more person breaks into spontaneous musical numbers, I swear I'm going to summon Cerberus just to eat the instruments."

Zeus was tangled in a vine again, yelling about how his peignoir was caught on an enchanted lute. Dionysus was serenading a boulder, convinced it was a dryad. The boulder, surprisingly, seemed flattered.

Arexia squinted.

"They're... enjoying this?" she said flatly. "That bard trap was supposed to drive them insane with discordant melody and emotionally repressed rhyming schemes."

The mirror shifted again, Sparkles had fashioned himself a judge's chair and was holding up a scorecard for Hercules's dance moves.

"Eight for effort," Sparkles declared. "Minus two for jazz hands."

Arexia's eye twitched.

"Fine," she muttered. "They think this is a talent show?"

She stood, swirling her stardust tea into a small tornado and smirking.

"Let's see how they handle a beast who only understands off-key yodelling and passive-aggressive slam poetry."

She waved her hand.

Somewhere in the next Realm, a monster awoke, annoyed, musical, and very, very loud.

And in the mirror, Arexia grinned.

"Let the Battle of the Bards begin."

Chapter Fifteen: Battle of the Bards and the Beast of Bad Harmony

It didn't roar like a monster.

It screeched like a broken violin dragged through a megaphone made of regret.

The Beast of Bad Harmony was fifty feet of snarling musical abomination harp strings for claws, flute pipes for teeth, cymbals strapped to its elbows, and a tail made of tambourines that jingled with murder.

Sparkles screamed. But in key.

"We need to fight it!" Medusa shouted, ducking a bass clef spike that whizzed past her head.

"With *music? *" Hercules barked, raising a sword made of cello necks.

"*OF COURSE WITH MUSIC! *" Sparkles howled, leaping onto a floating piano shard like a Broadway pirate.

Sparkles starts an impromptu solo:
"This is the worst wedding band ever!"
He hurls the triangle at the beast, which eats it and burps a dissonant G#.

Whiffles, kazoo blazing, performs a surprisingly potent distraction dance that causes the beast to trip on its own jazz hands.

Hera weaponizes passive-aggressive harp chords that temporarily freeze the beast's right side with guilt.

Zeus throws lightning in time with a beat drop.

Hades conjures ghostly orchestra spirits who chant ominously in Latin for no discernible reason other than vibes.

Loki remixes the battlefield by shifting its key signature mid-fight, causing the beast to stumble in rhythm.

"You just made the monster miss a beat!" Medusa laughed.

"I do my best work in improvisational chaos," Loki winked.

Medusa takes centre stage.

Her lyre erupts in flames. Each strum burns a note into the air. Truth. Pain. Power.

She sings one line. Just one:
"This is what you made of me."

The beast recoils. It tries to echo her note and fails. Shatters. Implodes into stardust and memory, the discord unravelling in reverse.

Everyone's panting, bruised, but alive.

"I've battled titans, gorgons, and my ex-wife's dinner parties," Zeus muttered. "But that... was hell."

"Oh, look," Sparkles said, brushing off his jacket. "The curtain's rising."

Beyond the dissipating battlefield, a new path revealed itself.

A Realm of Mirrors. A glimmer. A laugh.

"Aurelya?" Medusa whispered.

"Or Arexia pretending again," Loki muttered. "Either way... the show must go on."

The stage was set. The next Realm was watching. And they had just stolen the opening number.

Interlude: Mud, Muscles, and Misbehaving Queens

The air was infused with rose quartz mist and the scent of enchanted eucalyptus.

Aurelya sighed and sank deeper into the celestial mud bath, her crown floating like a lazy halo beside her.

Arexia, lying beside her with cucumber slices over her eyes and a golden goblet in hand, smirked.

"They're probably fighting musical monsters by now."

"Mmm," Aurelya hummed. "I hope Sparkles remembered to warm up his triangle. He throws off the harmonics when he panics."

They both burst into laughter.

From the next room, a harp version of *Toxic* by Britney Spears wafted through the spa vents. It was Arexia's request. Obviously.

Two massage attendants muscular, shirtless, and possibly former gods of relaxation stood silently nearby, glowing with post-massage serenity and respectfully fanning the queens with palm fronds made of stardust.

"So, tell me again," Arexia said, sipping her drink. "Which one of the men tried to 'rescue' you first?"

"Hercules," Aurelya purred. "Sweet, sweaty, stubborn Hercules."

"Classic," Arexia said. "Mine was Odin. He offered me a goat."

They giggled like chaos incarnate.

Aurelya peeked through her lashes at one of the attendants.

"That one has excellent thumb pressure," she whispered. "He found a knot in my soul and banished it."

"That's because he used to be the god of foreplay," Arexia whispered back.

The attendant winked.

The mud glowed softly.

Aurelya stretched luxuriously.

"Do you think we should check on them?"

"Not until the next mimosa," Arexia replied.

"Agreed."

And somewhere, far beyond the spa's magical sound barrier, the realms trembled.

But in here?

The only battle was who got to pick the next playlist.

Chapter Sixteen: The Realm of Eternal Curtain Calls

The moment they stepped through the shimmering portal, the world changed.

A golden spotlight hit them. Applause roared from nowhere. Curtains whooshed open across endless stages, revealing mirror versions of themselves mid-monologue.

"Why does everything feel like interpretive Shakespeare?" Loki muttered, adjusting his suddenly sparkly collar.

"Because" Sparkles said, eyes wide with awe, "we've entered the Realm of Eternal Curtain Calls."

"Oh gods," Hera groaned. "It's theatre punishment."

The Rules of the Realm

A scroll unfurled mid-air, dramatically narrated by an invisible voice:

"Welcome to the Eternal Curtain Call. Here, all guests must complete their Assigned Scene of Inner Revelation™ before the curtain may fall."

"Failure to deliver an emotionally authentic performance will result in permanent stage residency. Thank you and break a leg."

The scroll burst into confetti.

"What does emotionally authentic mean?" Zeus frowned. "Do I have to cry on cue?"

"Yes," the air whispered. "And if you fake it, your stage resets."

"This is my worst nightmare," Hercules muttered.

"This is my best nightmare," Sparkles whispered, already in costume.

Scene Assignments

- Zeus must perform a dramatic soliloquy confessing all his secret underwear thefts. The crowd goes wild when he sobs about the lavender thong.

- Hera must host a tell-all monologue titled "When the Crown Wasn't Enough."

- Loki is cast in every role in a one-man play called "Trick Me Once, Shame on You." He insists on playing all characters with sock puppets.

- Hades is forced into a musical duet with his own shadow about abandonment issues. It's awkwardly moving.

- Hercules accidentally enters a tap-dancing competition and wins despite never learning to tap.

- Medusa is handed a script titled "The Queen's Heart is a Haunted Thing." She reads one line and the whole theatre goes silent.

"I didn't ask for power. I asked to be safe."

Thunderous applause.

A curtain falls.

And rises again.

Because the Realm of Curtain Calls isn't done with them yet.

Chapter Seventeen: Dressing Rooms and Dangerous Truths

The moment the stage lights faded, a new doorway appeared behind them glowing pink and trimmed with gold. A sign hung crookedly above it, blinking in cursive:

"Backstage: Where Truth Undresses You."

"Nope," Zeus said flatly. "Absolutely not. I draw the line at glittery trauma."

"You drew that line three thongs ago," Hera shot back, marching through the door.

The others followed, reluctantly.

Inside was a vast hallway lined with ornate vanity rooms each labelled with a god's name. Not their current names. Their real ones. The ones they hadn't spoken aloud since before thrones and wars and temples.

The air smelled like powdered roses and reckoning.

Each had a room. Each had to face it.

Hades stepped into his and found a mirror that showed him smiling. Younger. Holding Persephone's hand. Still mortal. Still whole. A voice echoed from nowhere: "You weren't meant to be a king. But you stayed anyway." He sat silently, the smile in the mirror refusing to fade.

Hercules entered a closet filled with all the heroic costumes people said he wore. None fit. At the back was a tunic stitched with blood, not glory. His first battle. The one he never talks about.

He closed the door gently and whispered, "I'm
not just their myth."

Zeus didn't get a mirror. Just a single stool.
A parchment on the wall read, "What would
your daughters say?"
He didn't sit.

Hera's room sparkled with crowns. Gold. Jade.
Ruby. None of them heavy enough.
At the centre sat a simple iron crown with
thorns woven through the band.
She placed it on her head and said, "Finally.
Something that fits."

Loki's room was full of mirrors that lied. Each
reflection showed a version of himself too
charming, too evil, too tragic.
He smashed each one until only his tired eyes
remained.
That one, he nodded at.

Medusa's room was quiet. Empty. No crown. No mirror. Just stillness.

And in the stillness, she heard her own voice, soft but firm.

"I am not what they turned me into. I am what I choose to be now."

They returned to the hallway, quieter now. Less adorned. But more whole.

At the far end, a curtain fluttered open without a breeze.

"Next stage," said Sparkles.

"Do we get a script this time?" Hercules asked.

"Where we're going," Loki said, grinning, "there are no scripts."

Chapter Eighteen: The Stage with No Script

The stage was circular. Limitless. Suspended in starlight.

No backdrops. No props. No script.

Only them standing at the centre with every version of themselves watching from the crowd.

Some cheering.

Some sneering.

Some waiting to take their place.

"I don't like this," Hercules said, glancing at the versions of himself with too many abs and zero trauma.

"I don't like that mine are all smirking like they know something I don't," Loki added.

The air shimmered and answered with a booming voice:

"This is The Stage with No Script. Here, your truth becomes your story. Speak carelessly, and it becomes canon."

"What if we say nothing?" Hera asked.

"Then nothing is remembered."

The amphitheatre echoed like a memory unravelling.

The Performance Begins

Hera stepped forward first.

"I am not just the goddess of marriage. I am the warning label."

The audience snapped their fingers in divine approval.

Hercules followed, arms crossed.

"I didn't ask to be worshipped. I just wanted the killing to stop."

Thunder rumbled. Some versions of himself applauded. One cried.

Hades spoke low.

"I never chose the Underworld. But I chose to stay. And I'll choose again."

Zeus looked out at the crowd of judgmental versions of himself kings, warriors, thunder-hurling heartthrobs, and emotionally unavailable storm dads.

He adjusted his collar, cleared his throat, and stepped forward into the centre of the stage.

"There's no shame," he said loudly, "in wearing a lavender-pink thong."

He paused. Let it land.

"And occasionally," he added, raising a single

regal brow, "a silk peignoir... if the mood calls for it."

Half the amphitheatre gasped.

The other half cheered.

Sparkles slow clapped in awe.

"Finally," Hera muttered, "he says something I can respect."

Then Medusa stepped forward.

The stage shifted beneath her feet stone cracking, roots growing, mirrors rising from the floor.

Each mirror held a version of her serpent-haired, veiled in gold, burning in prophecy, still mortal, already divine.

She said nothing.

She didn't have to.

Every mirror turned to face her… and bowed.

"Where's my line?" Sparkles whispered, looking around.

"Oh no. I'm the comedic relief, aren't I?"

"Yes," Loki said. "But you also get the best costume changes."

The stage flickered.

And then it went dark.

A single spotlight landed on Loki.

The silence dared him to speak.

He stepped into the light.

"Fine," he said. "I'll improvise."

Chapter Nineteen: A Script Written in Flames (Goat Edition)

The moment Loki spoke, the stage erupted.

Not metaphorically.

Literally.

Flames licked the edges of the amphitheatre. The mirrors shattered into smoke. The spotlight turned blood red.

"Well," Loki muttered, "that escalated faster than Zeus at a toga party."

The floor beneath them cracked like parchment set aflame, symbols of ancient lore twisting and rewriting themselves in real-time beneath their feet.

"This isn't part of the journey, is it?" Hercules asked, pulling Medusa back from the edge.

"It is now," she replied. "The Realms are rewriting."

From the centre of the flames rose a stone pillar etched in runes that shimmered between Norse and Greek, flickering like memory and prophecy fighting for dominance.

Hades squinted. "Those runes are… wrong. They're not fully Greek. Not fully Norse."

"They're both," Sparkles whispered. "And something else. Something… rewritten."

The pillar flared.

Words seared into the sky:

"THE FLAME THAT WAS FORGOTTEN SHALL BURN AGAIN."

Zeus's face drained of colour. "Oh no."

Hera folded her arms. "You forgot another flame god?"

"Technically," Zeus said, backing away, "he wasn't forgotten. He was… delayed."

"Delayed?" Medusa asked.

"You know," Loki said slowly, rubbing his temples, "I have been hearing strange echoes lately… like someone sobbing into mead and calling their goat the love of their life."

Cut to: Somewhere Else

A dusty tavern. Dimly lit. Smells of pine beer, goat hair, and delusion.

Odin sat slumped over a wooden table, one eye glazed, the other focused lovingly on his goat.

"Buttermunch," he murmured, stroking the goat's chin, "has anyone ever told you… you're the finest woman I've ever seen?"

The goat bleated with mild concern.

Every time Odin tried to stand, the tavern door shimmered, and he reappeared, back on the bar stool, with another pint in hand.

"We tried to trap him somewhere secure," Zeus muttered back on the stage. "I thought a looped tavern of eternal ale and goat affection was merciful."

"You stuck Odin in a magical Groundhog Day bar with his goat?" Hades asked, horrified and impressed.

"He was being difficult!" Zeus insisted.

Back on the Stage

The flames rose again.

The Mirror of the Realms cracked wide open above them a jagged split of memory and madness.

"Uh-oh," Sparkles whispered. "The goat's waking up too."

"Don't tell me it's magical," Medusa groaned.

"It might be the key to breaking the loop."

"Of course it is."

Interlude: Brawl at the Bottomless Mug (A Love Story?)

Dionysus burst through the tavern doors like a man with a mission and absolutely no coordination.

"MY FRIENDS!" he declared to a room of startled patrons. "I have arrived... wherever this is!"

The tavern was enchanted, in that way that made you question your sobriety. Fireplaces blinked. Ale mugs refilled themselves. And at the far end, seated atop a barstool like he'd been born on one, was Odin.

He didn't even look up. Just wrapped an arm tighter around his beloved companion.

"Buttermunch," he murmured, nuzzling the goat's furry cheek. "You're the only one who understands me."

Buttermunch blinked slowly. He was chewing something. Possibly regret.

Dionysus staggered over. "You!" he shouted at the goat, pointing dramatically. "You are the most radiant, divine enchantress I've ever laid eyes on!"

Odin narrowed his one good eye.

"She's mine, wine-boy."

"Love," Dionysus slurred, grabbing the goat's hoof, "knows no ownership. Let her choose!"

Buttermunch looked between them in horror.

And that's when the bar brawl began.

Chairs flew. Tankards were weaponized.
Someone yelled, "NOT THE PINEAPPLE!" and
no one knows why.
Dionysus flung himself across a table,
attempting a drunken serenade. Odin
responded by hurling a pickled egg with
Olympic precision. It bounced off Dionysus's
forehead and landed perfectly in his wine glass.

"YOU'RE JUST JEALOUS I CAN DO THIS!"
Dionysus howled and attempted a backflip.
He failed.

Buttermunch climbed onto a shelf to avoid the
chaos, his tiny goat face deadpan as Odin and
Dionysus dramatically wrestled for "her"
affections.

The barkeep, wiping down the bar like nothing was happening, muttered, "Third time this week."

"Back away, beard-daddy," Dionysus warned, pointing a shaky finger. "That angel in hooves is mine."

Odin rose slowly. "You wanna dance, grape boy?"

Then he launched himself over the bar.

What followed can only be described as a divine disaster: shattered mugs, broken chairs, one cursed fiddle solo, and a sentient broom that tried to intervene before giving up and sweeping itself into the corner to cry.

Someone shouted, "IS THAT A GOAT IN A

WIG?"

(It wasn't. Dionysus brought the wig.)

The tavern exploded in cheers, bets, and confusion.

Eventually, Odin grabbed Dionysus by the toga and yeeted him toward the nearest glowing mirror.

The god of wine vanished with a loud, "WHEEEEE!"

Odin, panting, clutched Buttermunch protectively. "He'll be back," he grumbled. "They always come back for her."

Buttermunch bleated once. Long-suffering.

Meanwhile, Dionysus rolled out of a hedge in a completely different realm, covered in peanuts and crooning a love ballad to a shrub.

"Ohhh, spa day," he cooed, proudly reading the sign on the wall.

Chapter Twenty: The Goat, The Crack, and the Crown

Odin tried again.

One foot out the tavern door.

Freedom just one stride away.

"I will find my destiny!" he bellowed, slamming down his pint and stumbling out.

And

POOF.

Back on the stool.

Another pint.

Another bleat.

"Buttermunch," he whispered, "either I'm cursed... or you've bewitched me with those soft, judgmental eyes."

The goat blinked, unimpressed.

"I think this tavern is alive," Odin mumbled. "And it wants me to finish... my drink."

He clinked his pint against the goat's water bowl. "To fate."

Meanwhile, in the Mirror Realms...

The crack in the sky widened.

Not a tear a rift. The Mirror of the Realms shimmered between timelines, bleeding myths and chaos into each other like ink in water.

"Is it just me," Loki said, "or are the clouds shaped like goats?"

"That's a very specific hallucination," Hera replied.

A thunderclap sounded. Then...

A scream.

Followed by a goat bleat so haunting it silenced the sky.

"That's Buttermunch," Zeus whispered, eyes wide.

Medusa turned slowly. "You recognize a goat by sound?"

"I spent a lot of time with Odin," Zeus muttered. "There were many... evenings."

The Mirror pulsed.

And then

Odin fell through it.

Literally.

Right onto the centre of the flaming stage, tangled in goat, ale, and a crown that absolutely did not belong to him.

"Surprise!" he slurred. "I escaped destiny!"

Buttermunch landed on his head with a bleat of disdain.

"You brought the goat?" Hades asked.

"The goat brought me," Odin said proudly.

The flames flickered again.

A voice echoed from the cracked sky:

"THE CROWN IS MISPLACED. THE GOAT IS CHOSEN. THE REWRITE BEGINS."

Everyone turned to Buttermunch.

Sparkles narrowed his eyes. "...Is the goat about to become king?"

Interlude: We Heard There Was Mud

Somewhere between divine tantrums and spa-day serenity, the mirror shimmered again.

This time, it wasn't Arexia or Aurelya stepping through.

It was *drama. *

Persephone arrived first, dragging a suitcase that was somehow both floral and on fire. "I *knew* they'd be here without us," she muttered. "And I told Hades the next time there's a secret girls' day, I'm crashing it with vengeance and a rose clay mask."

Aphrodite followed, sunglasses already on despite being indoors. She held a mimosa in one hand and a suspiciously sharp nail file in the other. "I brought exfoliating daggers. And passive aggression."

The spa attendants looked up and immediately looked away.

They knew better.

"Reservation under...?" the receptionist tried.

"Under *divine right, *" Persephone snapped, tossing a pomegranate onto the desk that burst into glitter and judgment.

Moments later, they were in robes, oils slathered, toes soaking in golden honey foot baths.

Aurelya blinked when she saw them.

"Did you just appear through a mirror portal too?"

Aphrodite sipped her drink. "Darling, we *are* the mirror portal."

Arexia didn't even question it. She simply passed them a mocktail and said, "Welcome. We've already hexed the steam room to smell like victory."

The four of them clinked glasses.

And the spa day levelled up to something Olympus would *never* recover from.

Chapter Twenty-One: Mud, Magic & Mocktails

"Do you think they're still chasing us?" Aurelya asked, toes wiggling under a seaweed wrap.

Arexia didn't answer right away. She was levitating, suspended in a slow spin above a bubbling mud pool like an enlightened lizard in luxury.

"Let's see," she said, finally. "I offered them one portal clue, two monster distractions, a fog of forgetfulness, and a goat loop spell. They'll be busy."

Aphrodite sipped from a bright purple cocktail with a flamingo straw. "Honestly? I hope they never find us. I've never been this exfoliated in my immortal existence."

"You know it's serious," Persephone added, "when even I feel relaxed. And I rule a realm of the dead."

The spa air shimmered with magic. Towels folded themselves. Bubble masks sang elevator music. And one mirror tile in the wall flickered with a view of the Realms...

Sir Sparkles' face appeared, upside down and panicked.

"HELLO? LADIES? THE GOAT IS KING. I REPEAT - THE GOAT IS KING!"

The women blinked.

"Did he say the goat?" Aurelya asked.

"I knew Zeus left Odin unsupervised again," Arexia muttered, flipping midair.

The mirror went fuzzy.

A new spa bot rolled past with a tray of lavender mocktails and glitter-dusted cucumber slices.

"We'll deal with it after the mud soak," Arexia said, settling back with a sigh. "Let the Realms enjoy their little panic."

Interlude: Beast Mode, Spa Heist & Thong-Related Sabotage

The forest was not silent.

It roared.

With fire. With teeth. With something that definitely shouldn't have three heads, twenty-seven tentacles, and a fondness for riddles.

Hercules was the first to charge.

"NOT THE TENTACLES AGAIN!" he screamed as one wrapped around his leg like a clingy ex.

Loki skidded past, flinging enchanted glitter bombs. "This isn't the kind of group bonding I envisioned!"

Medusa launched herself into the fray, blade blazing. She ducked, spun, sliced through a vine that was definitely trying to spank her.

"WHY IS IT GROWLING IN RHYME?" she shouted.

"BECAUSE IT'S CURSED WITH POETRY!" Sparkles yelled from above, riding on a flying pinecone.

Meanwhile, Zeus wasn't even *there. *

Because two minutes earlier...

He'd fallen through a spa mirror.

To be fair, it had shimmered suspiciously but so did most things Zeus touched. One moment he was reaching for a foot mask left on a divine tray, the next he was tumbling face-first into a eucalyptus-scented paradise.

He sat up in a pile of cucumber slices.

"Am I dead?" he asked, brushing rose petals from his hair. "Or is this Elysium?"

A spa attendant blinked at him. "Sir, you are not scheduled for a treatment."

"I am now."

What followed was a very quick robe theft, a disastrous encounter with a massage table, and the quiet pilfering of a pink velvet pouch labelled: **"Property of Spa Day Do Not Remove." **

He'd just stuffed it in his robe pocket when the mirror behind him rippled again.

And *yeeted* him back out.

Mid-air.

He flew through the battlefield, crash-landing near Loki with a pouch in one hand, a glitter bomb in the other, and one slipper mysteriously missing.

"YOU'RE WEARING THE THONG AGAIN?!" Hades bellowed, mid-strike.

"It's LUCKY!" Zeus yelled back, only half-conscious, as a lightning bolt zapped his own hair.

The monster exploded.

Purple fire. Confetti. A smell of toasted marshmallows and monster tears.

And from a tree branch above

Came *laughter. *

The girls had seen it all.

In their matching spa robes, still covered in shimmer oil and holding fresh mocktails, they burst into giggles.

"Zues is wearing a thong!" Aphrodite shouted.

"You said you *lost* it!" Persephone snorted.

"It's not mine!" Aphrodite's Laughed, Slapping Persephone.

Zeus blinked, dazed. "Is this part of the massage?"

No one answered.

Because behind him, the tail of the beast twitched one last time…

And wrote a haiku in the dirt:

*Thongs are not weapons. *
*But they distract battle gods. *
*Spa day wins again. *

Chapter Twenty-Two: The Monster, The Muddle, and the Mystery Underwear

They stood in silence.

The beast had exploded.

Literally.

Chunks of shimmering fur and scales rained from the sky like confetti at a pyromaniac's birthday party.

"I don't know what it was," Hercules panted, brushing goo off his chest, "but I never want to fight something with three heads and a sudoku addiction again."

"It tried to *teach* me math mid-battle," Loki growled. "That's cruelty."

Medusa wiped monster ash off her blade. "Who summoned it?"

All eyes slowly turned to Zeus, who was trying to hide something behind his back.

"What's that?" Sparkles asked.

"Nothing."

"Is it glowing?"

"Define glowing," Zeus said, sweating.

He held out the object.

It was a pouch.

A radiant pink velvet pouch.

With embroidered letters:

'Property of Spa Day Do Not Remove.'

"You STOLE spa products?" Medusa asked, jaw dropping.

"I *rescued* them," Zeus defended. "You never know when a hydrating mist can save lives."

Loki snatched the pouch and dumped it out.

A bottle of shimmer oil, a charmed foot mask, and

“Are those your lavender-pink *thong underwear* again?” Hades asked, aghast.

“There’s no shame in comfort,” Zeus huffed. “Or lace. And occasionally a peignoir, if the mood calls for it.”

A long silence followed.

Then a crunch in the woods.

Another beast approached.

“Quick,” Sparkles said. “Throw the underwear at it. Maybe it’ll be blinded.”

Chapter Twenty-Three: The Crown, the Clone, and the Cringe

The second beast didn't attack right away.

It just... stared.

At Zeus.

More specifically, at the thong in his hand.

Medusa squinted. "Is it... confused?"

"No," Loki said grimly. "It's judging."

The beast smaller than the last but ten times more offended let out a deep, guttural sigh.

It turned around.

And walked away.

Everyone stood frozen.

"...Did we just get snubbed by a murder beast?" Sparkles whispered.

Zeus looked wounded. "I feel emotionally rejected."

"I feel validated," Hades said. "Finally, something with standards."

But the moment of peace didn't last.

Because from behind the trees came the sound of... applause.

Slow. Icy. Deliberate.

Arexia.

Standing atop a branch in shimmering boots, sipping a mocktail and twirling a parasol made entirely of regret and rhinestones.

"Oh, bravo," she purred. "You survived the Beast of Existential Despair. And the Sudoku Hydra. And the Flaming Karaoke Worm. You must be so proud."

"You sent the math monster?" Medusa snapped.

"Technically, I unleashed it," Arexia said with a wink. "Big difference."

Loki crossed his arms. "What's next? A tax demon?"

Arexia beamed. "Oh no. Much worse."

She snapped her fingers.

The sky cracked.

And from above floated...

Medusa?

No. Another Medusa.

But this one wore shimmering armour, a crown of mirrored scales, and an expression of absolutely zero emotional baggage.

Medusa stared. "What... is that?"

"Your potential," Arexia said sweetly. "Well,

one version of it. You know, the one who didn't fall in love with morally flexible gods and develop a crown complex."

The Other Medusa stepped forward, perfect posture and perfectly dead inside.

"I am Medusa Prime," she said. "You may call me Majesty."

Loki muttered, "She sounds like if a Pinterest board became sentient."

Hercules blinked. "She's... kinda hot though."

Medusa rolled her eyes. "Of course you'd say that."

Zeus coughed. "Can we throw the thong at this one?"

"No," Sparkles said. "It might join her outfit."

Arexia clapped again. "Let's see how you handle facing yourself, darling. Maybe then you'll understand the true price of rewriting the Realms."

And with that, she vanished in a poof of glitter.

Leaving Medusa staring down her doppelgänger.

And her doppelgänger... smiling like she already knew how this ended.

Chapter Twenty-Four: The Beast, The Blush, and the Betrayal Balm

The second beast was... confused.

Not just by the lavender thong fluttering in the air like a cursed battle flag, but by the collective group now standing before it, glitter-covered, spa-oiled, and emotionally unstable.

It sniffed.

Then sneezed.

A lot.

"Aromatherapy overload," Sparkles diagnosed, dabbing shimmer oil from his brows.

The creature this one only had two heads, mercifully shuffled back into the clearing. One head drooled. The other tried to braid its own ear.

Medusa readied her blade again, but Zeus stepped forward, dramatically flinging his peignoir over one shoulder.

"Let me try diplomacy."

"No!" yelled literally everyone.

But it was too late.

Zeus approached the beast with slow, exaggerated movements and a bottle of enchanted spa mist held aloft.

"I am Zentheus, god of radiance and

regeneration," he proclaimed. "Be soothed by the balm of betrayal and bergamot."

The creature's heads blinked. Then howled.

It charged.

"RUN!" Medusa shouted.

They scattered. The beast barrelled after them like a confused steamroller with an exfoliation kink.

"YOU PROMISED THIS WAS OVER!" Hercules bellowed.

"I thought it was!" Zeus wheezed. "Maybe it's allergic to betrayal balm!"

Loki popped out from behind a boulder. "Then

let's betray it harder."

He launched one of Zeus's thong underwear like a sling bullet. It hit the creature between the eyes.

It paused.

Stared.

Snorted.

Then curled up and went to sleep.

No one moved.

The forest held its breath.

A leaf fell.

The creature snored.

"...What just happened?" Hades whispered.

Sparkles tiptoed over, peered at the beast, then turned to the group.

"I think it... felt seen."

Zeus looked deeply moved. "It was longing for soft textures and emotional closure."

"No, it was longing for a nap and it got hit in the face with laundry," Medusa said.

"I am a healer of beasts," Zeus announced proudly.

"You are a thief of spa pouches and emotional dignity," Hades snapped.

Sir Sparkles raised a hand. "Can we just can we go five minutes without underwear trauma?"

Suddenly, the sky above them cracked.

Not thunder. Not lightning.

A voice.

A cold, glittering, very smug voice.

"Well," said Arexia, echoing through the Realm like champagne poured over ice. "They are making progress..."

Loki looked up. "Oh no."

"...Too much progress."

The air grew still.

Then the trees moved. Not swayed moved.

One unfurled into a staircase. Another bent into a spiral. The entire forest twisted like origami designed by a drunk architect.

"Okay," Sparkles muttered. "That's new."

Arexia's voice returned.

"Let's make things... interesting."

Zeus groaned. "I don't like when she says that."

Medusa gripped her blade tighter.

"I do."

Then the ground beneath them shifted. And the forest of chaos began to reshape once more.

Chapter Twenty-Five: Of Curses, Cucumber Slices, and Catastrophes

The forest had quieted. Too quiet.

Medusa, still holding Zeus's glitter-dusted pouch at arm's length like it might explode again, muttered, "If one more enchanted skincare product tries to kill me, I'm switching to mud masks and giving up."

Behind her, Hercules was attempting to use a monster scale as a mirror.

"It brings out my shoulders," he mused.

"No," said Loki flatly.

"You didn't even look!"

"I didn't have to."

Suddenly, a scroll flew through the air and slapped Sparkles in the face.

"Prophecy incoming!" he yelled, peeling it off his horn.

The scroll unrolled midair, glowing with ominous shimmer. It read:

"The balm that betrays, the blush that blinds,
Will turn the Realms, and twist all minds."

"That sounds bad," said Medusa.

"That sounds *fabulous*," said Arexia, stepping out from behind a tree as if she'd just returned from brunch with destiny.
The others jumped.

"Stop doing that!" Hades barked.

"I go where I'm needed," Arexia said smoothly, brushing an invisible speck from her shimmered cape. "And sometimes where I'm not. Like a good contour line."

Zeus backed up instinctively.

"You *are* behind this!" Medusa accused. "The beast, the spa pouch, the poem"

"I don't *cause* chaos," Arexia said. "I accessorize it."

Loki narrowed his eyes. "Then what does the balm do?"
Arexia's smile widened. "Why don't you try it and find out?"

She tossed a tiny glass jar into the air. It twirled once, sparkled, and landed in Medusa's palm.

The label read:
"Betrayal Balm™ – For when trust just isn't trending."

Sparkles squinted. "Does it do what I *think* it does?"

"Only if applied near the lips," Arexia winked. "Or the truth."

Before anyone could protest, the jar hissed and popped open, releasing a puff of rose-scented chaos.
Medusa flinched.

"Oh no," she said, already feeling it.

"What?" asked Hercules, stepping toward her.

Medusa's eyes were wide. "I... I want to tell you something... but I also want to slap you. Emotionally."

Arexia clapped. "It's working!"

Zeus groaned. "We're going to die smelling like a department store."

"Not if I have anything to say about it," Loki muttered, already pulling out a vial labelled "Anti-Betrayal Lip Scrub."

Everyone stared.

"What? I plan ahead."

And from the trees, the laughter of the Realms echoed once more.

Interlude: Spa Day Crasher (and the Cocktail Conspiracy)

Dionysus burst through the glimmering spa portal like a drunken cannonball wrapped in velvet.

"HELLO, GODDESSES," he announced, shirt half-missing, eyebrows singed, and clutching a flute made entirely of cheese. "I have ARRIVED."

The music stopped.

The spa, previously a haven of tranquillity and cucumber water, now smelled faintly of mead, glitter, and goat.

"Who let *him* in?" Persephone hissed,

adjusting her crown of seasonal foliage. "There's a *strict* no-chaos policy on the door."

"I *enchanted* the door," Dionysus beamed proudly. "Also, the drink concierge. Her name is Lucinda now. She brings me things."

As if summoned, a crystal-eyed nymph skated by, offering everyone iridescent cocktails and tiny cupcakes that whispered compliments when bitten.

Aphrodite glared at her empty glass. "He stays."

"Absolutely not," Persephone snapped. "Last time he joined a retreat, we ended up summoning a sentient disco ball and three emotionally needy centaurs."

Arexia tilted her head, amused. "And yet... I'm

intrigued."

"I brought offerings!" Dionysus slurred, producing a basket filled with olives, a bronze mirror, and a goat that may or may not have followed him from the last interlude.

"Is that Buttermunch again?" Aurelya asked, squinting. "He's wearing... is that a *mud mask*?"

The goat bleated smugly. Spa treatment acquired.

Dionysus immediately flopped into the nearest jade-tiled hot tub with a dramatic sigh. "So, ladies... what's new in realm-threatening chaos?"
Arexia passed him a glass without breaking eye contact. "You're late. We're already winning."

Aurelya sipped her drink. "We were just discussing who should take credit."

Dionysus nodded solemnly. "I accept your praise."
From across the spa, Whifflina sighed and scribbled frantically in the 'Spa Day Incident Log.' Line 438 now read:
"Dionysus crashed the spa. Again. May require divine locksmith."

Persephone crossed her arms. "He doesn't even have an appointment."

"I *am* the appointment," Dionysus whispered, raising a cucumber slice to the heavens. "Now... who wants a blessed mojito?"

Aphrodite reached for one. "Okay, he can stay.

For now.”

“ONLY if he stops singing love songs to the loofah,” Persephone warned.

Dionysus winked at the loofah. “No promises.”

Interlude: The Goat, the Thong, and the Tragedy of Taste

The camp was calm. Too calm.

Birds chirped. The fire crackled. Someone was roasting marshmallows with a cursed stick that occasionally screamed. All was peaceful.

Until Buttermunch found the lavender-pink thong.

He'd fished it out of Zeus's enchanted spa pouch which had been carelessly left open near a bush and was currently trotting around the camp like a champion, the thong dangling from his mouth like a victory flag.

Zeus noticed first.

"NOOO!" he screamed, leaping across the fire pit. "That's *limited edition! *"

Buttermunch bleated with pure chaos and bolted.

Odin gave chase, arms flailing. "That's my goat! You can't just *manhandle* a goat mid-snack!"

"You're supposed to keep him on a leash!" Zeus shouted.

"He's a free-range companion!" Odin roared back.

The two gods collided with a crunch of pride, glitter, and goat hair, tumbling into a full-on wrestling match over goat etiquette and undergarment rights.

"Are they fighting *again? *" Medusa asked, not even looking up from her scroll.

Sparkles sighed. "It's the passion for accessories that gets me."

"I think they genuinely believe Buttermunch is a sentient laundry thief," Loki added, munching popcorn conjured from thin air. "Which is hilarious because... *he kind of is. *"

Buttermunch zigzagged through the chaos, thong still flapping from his mouth, before tripping on a rock and, in one heroic chomp, swallowing it.

Everyone froze.

Zeus shrieked.

Odin dropped to his knees. "NOOOOOOOO! He ate it! He *ate* the unwashed thong!"

Watching from the spa "That poor goat," Persephone whispered. "No creature deserves such a fate."

"HE'S GOING TO GET SICK!" Odin wailed, clutching Buttermunch like a wounded soldier. "It was *unwashed! * It had... *body oil* on it!"

Loki coughed. "Well. At least it wasn't your peignoir."

Then, from the corner of the camp, Hera calmly walked over. Without saying a word, she reached into her divine purse and pulled out... a yellow thong.

Silk. Embroidered. Folded like royalty.

"Here," she said to Zeus. "Spare. I figured you'd need it."

Zeus took it reverently, eyes misty. He wiped his face with it, then turned to Hera and kissed her hand.

"I would be nothing without you."

She raised an eyebrow. "I know."

Behind them, Buttermunch let out a burp that shimmered with residual shimmer oil and poor choices.

The group stared.

Then Sparkles clapped once. "I propose we never speak of this again."

Loki grinned. "Too late. I already wrote a ballad."

Chapter Twenty-Six: The Map That Was Definitely Upside Down

The group stood on a hill shaped like a mildly concerned cupcake.

"This realm makes me nervous," Sparkles said, eyeing a suspiciously twitching flower.

"You're a walking disco unicorn," Loki replied. "You make *this* nervous?"

Hercules yanked the Realm Map from his bag. It immediately exploded into glitter, slapped Zeus across the face, and landed upside down.

"Why is it sticky?" Hades asked, peering over Medusa's shoulder.

"It was drawn by Bartholomew the Tiny," Sparkles said solemnly. "He's three. And prophetic."

"It's crayon," Medusa confirmed. "And maple syrup. With are those teeth marks?"

Before anyone could fix it, the map glowed violently and began to scream.

"Why is the map *singing*?" Zeus shouted.

"It's a performance map," Loki muttered. "You have to let it finish."

The scroll belted out a show tune about destiny and confusion, then projected a shimmering path in the air shaped like a question mark doing a cartwheel. The title scrawled across the top:

"WELCOME TO: The Carnival of Crippling Choices™"

Zeus blinked. "That feels personal."

"I hate this realm," Medusa muttered. "It smells like regret and novelty churros."

Suddenly POOF.

Dionysus appeared in a puff of rose-scented mist, wearing a gold silk robe and holding two cocktails.

"HELLO, MY DELICIOUSLY MISPLACED MISFITS."

Everyone froze.

"Where did *you* come from?" Hades asked.

"Odin threw me through a mirror," Dionysus said proudly. "Then Persephone and Aphrodite kicked me back through another one."

Loki narrowed his eyes. "So... you *know* how to get back to Spa Day?"

Dionysus sipped. "Darling, I *accidentally* invented three new spa treatments before they threw me out. I enchanted the drink concierge.

They're still getting unlimited foot scrubs in my name."

Sparkles gasped. "He knows the route."

Zeus sighed. "Our fate depends on a drunk man in a bathrobe."

Loki clapped. "This is finally getting interesting."

The map spun dramatically and tried to re-roll itself like it was too overwhelmed to continue.

"Don't worry," Dionysus said, patting it. "I once guided a whole theatre troupe to safety using interpretive dance. I've got this."

Hades leaned over to Medusa. "We're all gonna die, aren't we?"

Medusa nodded. "But at least our journey has snacks now."

Chapter Twenty-Seven: The Quest of Questionable Directions

The group now reunited-ish, thanks to Dionysus falling through multiple mirrors and spa-day portals like a wine-soaked GPS stood at the edge of a realm none of them recognised.

"I thought you said this was the shortcut to Arexia," Medusa said, arms folded.

"It is," Dionysus replied, upside down in a shrub. "According to the map. Which I may have been holding backwards. And possibly reading in mirror-script."

Sparkles floated beside him, unimpressed. "You followed a map written in crayon."

"Crayon of destiny," Dionysus corrected,

producing the aforementioned map. It smelled like fruit punch and poor decisions.

The terrain ahead was not ideal. A swamp, but make it dramatic bubbling mud ponds, suspiciously musical frogs, and the occasional vine that tried to braid your hair without consent.

Loki stared at a tree that was very clearly whispering insults. "If one more piece of nature judges me, I swear I'll set it on fire."

Aphrodite, who had reluctantly left spa day after being denied a sixth complimentary foot massage, looked around and sighed. "We could've stayed with cucumbers on our eyes. Now I have mud in my sandals."

Hercules squinted at the trail ahead. "Are

those… riddling otters?"

"Yup," Dionysus said cheerfully. "Answer wrong, and they make you do interpretive dance. Forever."

Hera blinked. "Why would Arexia put this on the path to her spa?"

"She likes to test people's emotional boundaries," Loki said, dodging a vine that tried to hug him aggressively.
Suddenly, Buttermunch bleated and trotted toward a glowing crystal path none of them had noticed before. The crystals pulsed with soft light and seemed to hum a vaguely Beyoncé-esque tune.

"Is the goat leading us?" Hera asked, incredulous.

"He's very intuitive," Odin sniffed, still sulking over the thong incident.

Sparkles shrugged. "Well, when in doubt, follow the magical goat."

And so, they did.

Into the swamp of confusing choices, whispering vines, interpretive otters, and one very sassy goat wearing a crown of wildflowers.

Medusa narrowed her eyes. "We're getting close. I can feel it."

"And I can feel that something ridiculous is about to happen," Loki muttered.

Because, of course, it always does.

Chapter Twenty-Eight: The Realm of Optional Dragon Attacks

They emerged from the swamp like survivors of an interpretive dance battle and in some cases, they were.

Medusa's braid was twitching with residual rage. Hera had vines in her crown. Loki had somehow acquired a glitter moustache. No one asked how.

"Is it just me," Sparkles said, shaking swamp water off his fur, "or did that last otter imply I have unresolved issues with my mother?"

Dionysus flopped dramatically onto a rock. "That's because you do."

Before Sparkles could conjure a rebuttal, the sky cracked open.

Literally.

A jagged seam tore across the clouds, and through it came a deep, echoing roar.

"That," said Hades, stepping forward, "was either a dragon… or my ex-wife."

"I thought Persephone was here with us," Hercules whispered.

"She is," Hades replied. "Which is why I'm now terrified."

Flames licked the edge of the forest ahead. The trees weren't burning, they were applauding. Literally. Little branches clapped excitedly.

"I think they're happy to see us," Loki said, suspicious.

"No," said Medusa. "They're excited because they know something we don't."

A shadow crossed the ground.

Then another.

Then three more.

A dragon the size of a small mountain swooped overhead, followed by two smaller dragons, one with a bowtie.

"AREXIA!" Sparkles shouted into the sky. "STOP SENDING US STUFF!"

A floating mirror shimmered to life beside them. Arexia's voice came through, cheerful and vaguely condescending.

"You're welcome! Optional dragon attack initiated. You can skip it, but only if you answer the riddle correctly."

"Oh no," Hera muttered. "Not riddles again."

"Goat!" Odin called. "Do you know the answer?"

Buttermunch trotted up to the mirror and bleated once.

The mirror blinked.

Correct answer accepted.

The dragons vanished in a puff of glitter and disappointment.

Everyone turned to the goat.

"What did he say?" Medusa asked.

Sparkles translated: "He said, 'Your riddle was stupid.'"

They stood in stunned silence.

Then Dionysus clapped. "I *love* this goat."

The mirror fizzled out. A new path lit up this one lined with enchanted topiaries shaped like their worst fears.

"Who the hell designed this place?" Hades asked.

"A goddess with flair," said Aurelya, finally rejoining them with her spa-day glow still radiating.

The group pressed forward, past mocking shrubs and judgmental bushes.

Because somewhere ahead, Arexia waited.

And she was *enjoying* every second of this nonsense.

Interlude: The Shimmering Return (And a Mildly Judgy Bush)

Aurelya strolled through the swamp like it was a red carpet.

Her hair still carried the faint scent of enchanted rose oil. Her skin glowed like she'd made out with a moonbeam. Her nails sparkled with stardust polish in a hue called "Otherworldly Confidence."

She hummed a spa-day tune as she stepped delicately over a puddle of suspicious goo that had tried to eat Loki's boot five minutes earlier.

A vine slithered toward her. She stared at it.

It recoiled.

"I told you," Aurelya said to no one in particular, "exfoliate with intention, and the world obeys."

Behind her trailed a glittering mist that smelled of cucumber water, validation, and barely repressed chaos.

A talking bush near the path scoffed. "Oh look, glitter girl's back."

Aurelya didn't break stride. She tossed a single glowing cucumber slice onto its leaves and whispered, "Hydrate."

The bush went silent, overcome with dewy clarity.

Meanwhile, up ahead, the group was knee-deep in swamp despair. Aphrodite was attempting to wring out her hair using only judgment. Hera was muttering about cursed sandals. Dionysus had attempted to drink the swamp and was now glowing green.

Aurelya appeared behind them like a spa-summoned vision.

"A goddess with flair," she said, beaming.

Everyone turned.

"You're glowing," Hercules blinked.

"Inside and out," she confirmed.

Loki looked down at his mud-caked boots. "I hate everything."

Aurelya twirled once, then joined the party as if

nothing had happened because when you're
that radiant, no one questions your entrance.

Not even the whispering vines.

Chapter Twenty-Eight: The Bridge, the Bribe, and the Surprisingly Rude Moss

The path led them straight into a clearing that should've been peaceful if not for the moss screaming insults in five different languages.

"You call that a tunic?" one patch yelled at Zeus.
"Nice muscles, shame about the brain," another added for Hercules.

"Is the foliage negging us?" Aphrodite asked, horrified.

"It's enchanted moss," Sparkles said, poking a tuft that promptly insulted his wing shape.
"Very insecure. Projects a lot."
Up ahead, a glittering crystal bridge floated in

midair just floated, no railings, no ropes, no visible means of support.

"Don't like that," Hera muttered.

"I do!" Dionysus beamed, stepping forward and immediately tripping over Buttermunch's tail. The goat gave him a look and resumed chewing a flower crown that may or may not have been sacred.

A figure appeared at the centre of the bridge. Tall. Cloaked. Radiating smugness.

"Who dares seek passage to the realm beyond?" boomed the figure.

Medusa stepped forward. "We do."

"You must answer my questions three, or pay

the toll," the figure said ominously.

Loki sighed. "Let me guess. If we fail, we fall into the sparkly abyss?"

The figure nodded.

"I vote bribe," Zeus said, fishing in his pouch. "What do rude moss and bridge gremlins want these days? Gold? Thongs?"

"NO," everyone shouted.

Hercules flexed. "Or we could fight."

Sparkles raised a paw. "Violence is not always the answer, unless the question is 'What's the Realmsverse's favourite hobby?'"
The figure held up a hand. "You may not bribe. You may not fight. You must earn your way

across."

A long pause.

"Fine," Aurelya said, pulling out a glowing spa-day token. "I bribe the moss."

"...What?" the figure blinked.

She flicked the token onto the ground. The moss shimmered. Sparkled. Giggled.

Suddenly, the moss whispered sweet compliments and flattened into a smooth, mossy runway.

The bridge lowered.

The cloaked figure removed their hood, revealing... a teenage squirrel with dramatic eyeliner and a clipboard.

"You passed," it said, bored. "But like, barely."

"Was that squirrel wearing lip gloss?" Loki whispered.

"I think we just got judged by a woodland intern," Persephone added.

As they crossed the now-accessible bridge, Dionysus muttered, "I miss the riddle otters. At least they respected interpretive dance."

From behind them, the moss cooed:
"Walk that bridge, sparklekins. Slay."

And they did.

Interlude: Return of the Sass Queen (Now Featuring Swamp Monster Romance)

One moment, Persephone had been getting her hair wrapped in celestial vines by a bored dryad at the spa. The next?

Mirror.

Swoosh.

Swamp.

She landed gracefully well, mostly into a patch of moss that immediately judged her footwear choices.

"Rude," she muttered, brushing off her sandals, glitter still clinging to her like a VIP sticker from Spa Day.

She wandered forward, following the unmistakable sounds of chaos and arguing.

The group was crossing a moss-covered bridge that looked like it had feelings. It wobbled when insulted and whispered compliments if you said "please."

Persephone was about to call out when she noticed the group had split across perception lines.

To her left: Aphrodite, Aurelya, Dionysus, and Sparkles skipping (literally) over the bridge like it was a catwalk made of cupcakes. Birds chirped. Flowers sang. A frog offered high tea.

To her right: A very different scene.

Hercules was wrestling something that looked like a swamp hag mixed with a tentacle-themed nightmare.

"Oh gods," Persephone muttered, watching him press a chaste kiss to the creature's slimy cheek as it purred and dissolved into sparkles, clearing the path.

Medusa groaned. "Did he just?"

"Yup," Hades confirmed, cleaning goo off his boots. "Apparently that's the toll."

Ares poked a vine that tried to flirt with him. "I hate this place."

Persephone finally strolled up beside them, casually tossing her hair.

"Miss me?" she asked with a grin.

"Where did *you* come from?" Loki blinked.

"Mirror thing. Probably Dionysus' fault. Again." She glanced back at Hercules and raised an eyebrow. "So... we're kissing monsters now?"

"She was *very persuasive*," Hercules muttered, wiping sludge from his face.

"Darling, your standards have officially drowned in that bog," Persephone teased, patting his goo-slicked shoulder.

As the group continued across the now-unified bridge path, Aurelya reappeared too, radiant from her spa glow.

"A goddess with flair," she declared, joining the chaos like it was her runway.

Persephone tilted her head at the muttering shrubs.

"I think we just got judged by a woodland intern," she said dryly.

No one disagreed.

Chapter Twenty-Nine: The Bridge, The Sass, and The Swamp-Faced Truth

The bridge stretched before them like an overambitious catwalk narrow, winding, and suspended by what looked like threads of moonlight and moss. Below: swamp. Above: judgmental clouds. Beside them: chaos.

Loki stepped onto the bridge and immediately recoiled. "It's squishy. I don't trust squishy."

Persephone sashayed past him. "It's enchanted. Probably woven from ego and questionable life choices."

"But whose?" Aphrodite asked, poking the rail, which hissed and tried to bite her.

"Mine," Arexia's voice echoed softly from nowhere and everywhere. "Now walk."

Hercules took the lead. Confident. Heroic. Glowing just a little too proudly.

That's when the bridge shifted.

And from beneath it, rose a shape, a swamp creature with eyes like murky ponds and lips ready for regret.

"Oh no," Hera muttered. "Not another swamp trial."

The creature opened its mouth. "Only a kiss from a heart pure and slightly confused shall grant you passage."

Everyone turned to Hercules.

He blinked. "What? Why me?"

"You're the only one who looks like he'd kiss something with teeth and a skincare problem," Persephone quipped.

With a heroic sigh and a whispered apology to his dignity, Hercules leaned in and smooched the monster.

A loud squelch.

A shimmer of swamp goo.

And the bridge lit up, golden and solid.

"You kissed it!" Persephone shrieked in horror-delight. "You actually kissed it! Are you okay? Do you need a tetanus shot? A priest?"

The creature, now beaming, floated away humming something suspiciously romantic.

Hercules wiped his mouth, gagging. "I did it for the team."

"Sure," Aphrodite grinned. "But also... eww."

Sparkles fluttered past with his nose in the air. "Next time, we just sacrifice him and take the scenic route."

They pressed on.

Step by step, sass by sass.
And somewhere, far ahead, Arexia smiled.
Because the next trial wasn't about strength.

It was about secrets.
And which of them were ready to tell the truth.

Chapter Thirty: The Crown, The Crackle, and the Realisation That This Might've All Been a Bit Much

The bridge crackled beneath their feet literally.

Each step across the crystalline span made a sound somewhere between lightning and popcorn. Sparkles floated cautiously above it, muttering about unstable molecular harmonics and the importance of not stepping on the shiny bits.

"It's all shiny bits," Loki muttered.

Aurelya walked with regal calm, the soft glow of leftover spa bliss still clinging to her hair like she'd just walked out of a shampoo commercial.

"This place is beautiful," she said, ignoring the carnivorous vines and lurking swamp things. "It's like a fever dream and a Pinterest board had a baby."

"Don't give it ideas," Medusa warned. "The Realm might be listening."

They made it halfway across the bridge when it happened.

The sky if it could be called that shivered.

Above them, the Mirror of the Realms cracked again.

A jagged bolt of energy split the horizon, sending a pulse of magic so strong it nearly knocked Sparkles out of the air.

"Oh, that's not good," he squeaked.

"Define 'not good,'" Hera said, eyes narrowing.

The crack in the sky flickered, revealing glimpses of other timelines, moments past and future colliding in a kaleidoscope of what-the-heck.

They saw themselves.

Fighting. Falling. Failing.

Zeus as a llama.

"Don't look too long," Dionysus warned, adjusting his grapevine crown. "You might see spoilers."

The bridge began to sway.

Monsters stirred in the swamp below, their forms too unstable to name. One looked like it was made of failed childhood dreams. Another had the face of someone's ex.

The crackle intensified.

And then

BOOM.

A surge of energy exploded from the Mirror above, hitting the bridge and throwing everyone off their feet.

When the dust cleared, Medusa stood first, sword ready. "Roll call!"

"Here!" Loki coughed, pulling himself out of a bush that definitely hadn't been there a second ago.

"Sparkles still glowing," the pixie chirped.

"Zeus has landed in a heroic pose," Zeus announced, stuck halfway through a hedge.

Buttermunch bleated defiantly.

Aurelya straightened her spine, eyes fixed on the glowing path ahead. "We're close. I can feel it."

Loki grunted. "I can feel something too. Possibly internal bleeding."

The Mirror above them pulsed.

One final word shimmered across it:

CHOOSE.

They all looked at each other.

The choice was coming.

And it wouldn't be simple.

Chapter Thirty-One: Maze, Mirror, Mayhem (Again?)

They stood in silence.

Again.

Before them stretched the familiar (and entirely unwelcome) shimmering entrance to the Maze of Mirrors. Its glassy surface rippled like it knew they were coming and was laughing.

"Is it… broken?" Medusa asked, one eye twitching.

"No," Loki muttered, rubbing his temples. "It's worse. We've been here before."

"But we turned left at the swamp of emotional

otters," Hera insisted. "We *turned*!"

"Unless..." Sparkles drifted slowly through the air, antennae glowing with dread. "Arexia enchanted the map again."

Dionysus held up their current map, now pulsing softly in neon pink and shaped like a banana. "It *did* ask me to peel it earlier."

"I swear," Hercules growled, covered in moss and something that might have been toad spit, "if we have to interpretive dance our way through that mirror maze again, I'm fighting a fern."

"You already *did* fight a fern," Hades said. "It won."

Aurelya sighed, her spa-day glow slightly

dimmed. "This feels personal."

"Of course it's personal," Loki snapped. "This entire Realm was built by a woman who weaponised bath salts."

Zeus pointed at the mirrors, which now bore cheeky captions beneath each reflection:

- *You Tried.*
- *Still Not Hotter Than Dionysus. *
- *Warning: Emotional Reflection May Occur.*

Buttermunch bleated in solidarity. He had refused to look into the mirrors since the last time, when they showed him as a llama in a tutu. He hadn't been the same since.

"Look," Medusa said, massaging her temples, "we can't just stand here debating whether the mirrors are gaslighting us. We need a plan.”

“Oh! I have a plan!” Dionysus raised a hand enthusiastically. “We break the mirrors!”

Everyone stared at him.

“With what?” Hera asked.

“My emotional trauma.”

A pause.

“…He might actually be onto something,” Hades admitted.

Suddenly, one of the mirrors flickered. A new path appeared behind it, but only for a moment.

"Did anyone else see that?" Persephone asked, stepping forward.

"See what?" Aphrodite said, reapplying lip balm with a scowl. "I'm too busy trying not to scream. This was supposed to be a straight line. A straight line. To Arexia. What sort of goddess *loops* the same trauma?"

"The kind who thinks trauma is character development," Aurelya muttered.

"Or the kind who thinks we need to suffer a little more before the final spa treatment," Loki added grimly.

Odin was staring down at the enchanted banana-map. "The map just told me 'you're almost there'… in Comic Sans."
Zeus howled. "IT MOCKS US."

In the middle of the chaos, Buttermunch trotted toward the maze entrance, paused, and headbutted a specific mirror. It shattered harmlessly, and behind it was a hidden door.

"...Of course the goat figured it out," Hera said flatly.

"He's brilliant," Odin whispered, eyes brimming with tears. "He's my hero."

Sparkles clapped. "Well, gang. Time to follow the magical goat. Again."

Loki sighed, stepping over glittering shards. "I hate this place."

"I hate this quest," Persephone added.

"I hate everyone who isn't offering snacks,"

Dionysus mumbled.

And yet, one by one, they followed the goat. Into the maze. Again.

Back into the glimmering vortex of reflections, riddles, and the faint, ever-present sound of someone somewhere giggling at their misfortune.

And far above them, in her private spa chamber, Arexia sipped her drink and smiled.

"Let's see how they handle this round."

Interlude: The Spa That Stole the Quest

The Realm of Echoes had gone suspiciously quiet.

No monsters.
No labyrinths.
No screaming squirrels or fire feathers or reality-shattering mirror prophecies.
Just... steam. And the scent of lavender.

"Wait. Weren't we in the Maze of Mirrors two seconds ago?" Hercules asked, blinking at the polished marble around them.

"You say that like it's a bad thing," Ares grunted, already half-naked and reclining in the sauna, a towel draped low on his hips.

Loki lounged beside him, fanning himself dramatically with a palm frond he'd conjured out of nowhere. "Darling, if this is an illusion, I vote we stay. The humidity does wonders for my curls."

Hades cracked one eye open from his seat in the corner, a shadowy towel over his face. "We *should* be worried."

Meanwhile, in the mud baths, chaos was brewing.

"You goat-sniffing thunder dolt, he *ate* my thong!" Zeus bellowed, flinging a handful of mud at Odin.

"It was not I who fed the thong to the goat!" Odin roared back, beard splattered with mud, arms waving wildly. "Blame the temptress beast!"

Buttermunch the Goat, now sunk shoulder-deep in warm, scented sludge, blinked innocently. His jaw moved slowly.

Suspiciously.

Zeus gasped. "*He's still chewing it. *"

"I think he's traumatised," Dionysus muttered dreamily from the next tub, swirling his wine like it was aged prophecy. His cheeks were flushed, his smile wistful. "My sweet, slippery, sinful mud blossom... come back to me."

Buttermunch bleated and inched closer to Hera's foot spa.

"You *cannot* seduce the goat again," Medusa snapped at Dionysus, deadpan, as she reclined beside Hera and Persephone, feet soaking in rose petal–infused bubbles. "We've talked about this."

"I thought we were getting mani-pedis," Persephone sighed, inspecting her freshly glittered nails.

"We are," Hera said, not looking up. "Let Zeus and Odin mud-wrestle over goat thongs. This is the only peace I've had since Book One."

Back in the sauna, the steam thickened with bro tension.

"So how many monsters have *you* slain this week?" Ares challenged, stretching with a groan.

"Lost count," Hercules said smugly, flexing. "But I broke a Minotaur's femur with a single bicep curl, so..."

"Boys," Loki drawled, "let's not compare scars unless we're also comparing egos. Actually, never mind. That would take all eternity."

"Wait," Hades said suddenly, sitting up. "Why are we *relaxed*? We're *never* relaxed. Something's wrong."

"Wrong?" Loki blinked. "We've got cucumbers on our eyes and hellfire under our towels. What could possibly," He froze mid-sentence. "Oh no."

They all turned at once.

The air shimmered. The pedicures vanished. The mud turned cold. The wine glass cracked. And a single name whispered through the room like a forbidden spell.

"Arexia…"

Everyone jolted.

"WE FORGOT AREXIA!" Medusa stood up so fast the water sloshed from her tub.

"She's still out there!" Hera gasped.

"And we're in an *illusion*!" Hades growled, yanking off his towel like it offended the Underworld.

Buttermunch let out a tragic bleat, burped up a *single* lavender thread from the former thong, and fainted.

Zeus collapsed to his knees. "My beautiful... undergarment..."

"I *told* you," Odin huffed, arms crossed, "never trust a spa that hands out complimentary ambrosia shots."

The enchantment shattered with a pop of vanishing nail polish and exploded bath salts. Their mission snapped back into focus, and the steam was replaced with swirling winds and a too-familiar glint of mirrored corridors.

They were back in the Maze.

Zeus looked down at his ruined, mud-splattered thighs.

"I miss my thong."

Chapter 32: The Map That Lied and the Mirror That Laughed

They were back in the Maze.

And absolutely *no one* was happy about it.

"I swear this corridor had a left turn two hours ago," Persephone said, glaring at the shimmering wall in front of them.

"It did," Medusa muttered. "Now it's got a vending machine."

Everyone turned.

Indeed, where a mirrored hallway had once stood, a glistening golden vending machine hummed. It offered snacks like *"Prophecy Pretzels," "Time Loops in a Can," * and one suspicious button labelled simply: "Push For Regret."

"Don't push it," Hades warned.

Loki had already pushed it.

A small puff of glitter exploded in his face. "Okay, that was *mildly* regrettable," he said, blinking sparkles off his eyelashes. "I expected worse."

"You're holding a ferret now," Hercules noted.

Loki looked down. Indeed, in his arms was a small white ferret wearing a monocle and a tie. The ferret squeaked with disapproval.

"Okay," Loki said, handing the ferret to Ares like a hot potato. "I deeply regret that button."

"Why do we *keep* ending up in the same place?" Hera snapped, yanking the enchanted map from Hades's hand. "We've walked in circles."

"That's impossible," Zeus grumbled. "I've been tracking our path by the position of my mud stain."

"You mean that squiggle on your thigh that looks like Australia?" Odin asked.

"Exactly."

Medusa snatched the map from Hera and stared at it. The lines were shifting not slowly, not subtly. They *wiggled*. A corridor disappeared. A new one bloomed like a vine. An arrow labelled "You Are Here" smirked and twirled in a lazy circle.

"This isn't a map," she growled. "It's a mood ring with delusions of grandeur."

Suddenly, a voice echoed through the Maze, soft and lyrical, like silk over knives:

"Oh dear... You're lost again?"

It was Arexia. Or at least her illusion.

Her laughter trickled down the walls, curling like mist. The vending machine vanished. The mirror in front of them rippled and then laughed. Literally. The glass parted its shimmer like lips and chuckled.

"Did... did the mirror just *giggle* at me?" Hercules asked, taking a step back.

"Yes," Ares muttered, sword out. "And it winked."

"You know what this means," Persephone said grimly.

Loki raised a brow. "That we're deeply screwed?"

"No." Persephone pointed. "It means Arexia's changing the map to mess with our heads. She wants us to doubt the path."

"And it's working," Hades grunted. "I've never been this confused outside a family reunion."

Zeus rubbed his temples. "Okay, team meeting. Who *still* has the enchanted sock with the compass enchantment stitched by the Gnome of Direction?"

Everyone looked at Odin.

"I traded it," Odin confessed. "For two mangoes and a back scratch."

There was a beat of silence.

Loki blinked slowly. "This is why no one lets you handle treasure."

Medusa's hands clenched around the map. "Alright. We find a way forward. Together. No shortcuts. No vending machines. No ferrets. And no more enchanted detours unless it involves stabbing something helpful."

The ferret squeaked in agreement.

They turned toward the corridor with the fewest suspicious giggles and began to walk one step at a time, deeper into the Maze, the path behind them sealing shut with a sigh.

But somewhere, Arexia watched.
And the map giggled again.

Interlude: The Ferret Who Knew Too Much

No one knew his real name.

He'd been summoned by a button. Born of vending machine regret.

One puff of glitter and *poof* there he was.

White as snow, sharp as suspicion, and wearing a monocle with the quiet dignity of someone who once chaired a board meeting in a library.

They called him many things:

– The Glimmering Weasel of Mystery

– Sir Nibbleworth the Third

– Mr. Squeaks

– That Little Freak with Secrets

But only one name echoed in silence, whispered in fear by the most powerful magical creatures across the realms:

"The Ferret."

He adjusted his tie with the poise of someone deeply disappointed in everyone around him.

The group argued loudly over a mirrored fork in the corridor.

"Left!" yelled Hera.
"Right!" argued Odin.
"Snack break!" proposed Dionysus, who was holding a half-eaten hallucination.

The Ferret squeaked once.

Everyone ignored him.

He squeaked again, this time more insistently, pointing with his tiny paw toward a narrow tunnel hidden behind an illusory wall.

They all continued bickering.

Finally, with the exasperated sigh of someone who had already solved the maze twice, the Ferret scurried over to a patch of floor, tapped it with his paw, and vanished.

Medusa blinked. "Did the ferret just... teleport?"

Hades groaned. "We're being outmanoeuvred by a small rodent in formalwear."

"He's not just any ferret," Loki muttered, eyes narrowing. "He's the one from the prophecy."

"What prophecy?" asked Ares, frowning.

Loki hesitated. "Okay, technically, it was a riddle I found in a haunted crossword puzzle. But I'm pretty sure it mentioned a ferret in a tie."

Hercules crossed his arms. "You just want an excuse to chase after him."

Loki shrugged. "He has better fashion sense than most of us. I trust him."

Meanwhile, deep inside the maze, the Ferret emerged from the shadows.

He pressed his tiny paw to a mirror, and it opened.
Inside was a swirling memory vault of secrets Arexia never meant anyone to find.

He looked over his shoulder once. Then disappeared into the glass with a final, dignified squeak.

Back in the corridor, a scroll suddenly appeared in midair and bopped Zeus in the face.

"Ow!"

He unrolled it.

It read:

"Follow the Ferret. Or fail."

Signed,

– S.T.F. III (Sir Tiberius Ferretus the Third)

Loki grinned.

"I knew he had a name."

Chapter 33: The Corridor of Hidden Things

They didn't so much walk into the mirror as fall into it.

One second, they were staring at the scroll. The next, the mirror shimmered like a liquid laugh and swallowed them whole.

No screams.
Just the faint squeak of a ferret ahead of them, urging them deeper.

The corridor was nothing like the maze outside.

It wasn't made of stone, or glass, or even air.

It was made of memory.

Walls pulsed with old visions. Childhood. Betrayal. Mistakes they thought were buried.

The scent of first victories and last regrets clung to the edges like dew.

"This is... uncomfortable," Medusa muttered, brushing past a flicker of her former self, young, bright-eyed, before the gods had stolen her power.

Ares grunted. "Mine just showed me crying during a haircut."

"Mine played my karaoke performance from the Realm of Karaoke," Hercules said, horrified. "The notes were publicly off-key."

Hades passed a vision of himself reaching out for someone, Persephone, maybe, but she vanished before he could touch her.

Zeus turned pale as one wall displayed the memory of his lavender thong being eaten in slow motion. The goat had a soundtrack this time.

"I hate this place," he muttered.

Only Loki seemed unfazed.

He walked with his hands behind his back, whistling a jaunty tune, every once in a while, pausing to examine someone else's memory and comment helpfully:

"Oof. That haircut was a mistake."

"Did you really think that toga looked good on you, Hades?"

"Oh, look, it's me being right. Again."

"Loki," Medusa said through gritted teeth, "do you have any embarrassing memories?"

He smiled, but it didn't quite reach his eyes.

"Too many," he said softly. "But I edited mine to reruns. Perks of being chaos incarnate."

Then they saw it.

At the very end of the corridor, nestled between columns of smoke and light, was a pedestal.

And on that pedestal:
A map. But not just any map.

It was Arexia's map. The original. The unedited. The truth she was hiding.

Sir Tiberius Ferretus III stood guard at its base, tie slightly askew from the journey.

He gave a noble nod.

Medusa approached slowly. Her fingers hovered just above the parchment. The others crowded around.

The map shimmered then snapped into clarity.

Gasps echoed.

"It's not just the Maze," Persephone breathed.
"She's rewritten the entire Realm."

"She's erased paths," Hera whispered. "And people."

"Look at this," Hades muttered, pointing to the margins. "She's moved the Gate of Flame… she's hidden the Crowned Grove… she's-"

"Turned me into a background character," Loki said, scandalised. "I demand revenge and possibly a musical number."

But Medusa wasn't looking at any of them.

She was looking at a single name scrawled in bold, mirrored script across the heart of the map:

Andreas.

Her hand trembled.

"I knew it," she whispered. "I knew something was missing."

Everyone fell silent.

"She erased him," Medusa said, voice low, almost reverent. "I kept feeling it. This ache I couldn't name. The space beside me that used to feel... full. It wasn't grief. It wasn't longing. It was erasure."

Zeus frowned. "Who's Andreas?"

Medusa didn't answer.

The map pulsed.

The corridor began to shake.

Sir Tiberius Ferretus III squeaked twice and leapt onto Loki's shoulder.

"Time to go!" Loki yelled.

"Exit spell?" Zeus shouted.

"More like Exit Chaos," Loki grinned.

He snapped his fingers.

The corridor exploded into feathers and fog.

They landed hard back in the maze, gasping, sprawled, and blinking.

Medusa clutched the real map. The ferret adjusted his monocle.

They had the truth now.

And Arexia?

She had no idea they'd stolen it.

Yet.

Chapter 34: The Silence Between Shadows

They didn't speak for a long time.

Back in the twisting halls of the Maze, the group walked with new purpose but also a strange quiet. Not the silence of peace.

The silence of something dangerous returning.

Medusa gripped the true map like it was a lifeline. Her fingers trembled.

Andreas.

The name pulsed through her like an echo she hadn't realised she was chasing, until now.

"I knew it," she murmured again, more to herself than to them. "He was never gone. Just... erased."

The ache in her chest, the strange certainty that she had lost something vital, it all made sense now. It hadn't been longing. It had been absence. The kind so deep it warps the soul.

Even Loki, who usually filled silence with snark, said nothing.

They set up camp in a mirrored alcove that didn't reflect their faces, only versions of themselves that smiled too easily.

"It's a memory snare," Loki said quietly, eyeing the false smiles. "Don't look too long."

Hades tossed a shadow ward over the alcove. "She'll know we found something soon."

"Then we make a plan before she does," Medusa said. Her voice was flat steel now.

Ares crossed his arms. "Who is Andreas?"

Medusa looked down at the map. "He was mine. Before all of this. Before I became what they made me."

"A god?" Hera asked.

Medusa shook her head. "No. Mortal. Strong. Stubborn. He believed in me before I had claws to protect myself."

"You never mentioned him," Persephone said softly.

"I couldn't." Medusa's eyes shimmered. "Because I didn't remember. When I came through the Mirror... I knew I had to find Arexia. I felt it in my bones. But I didn't know why. I couldn't remember what she took."

Now she knew.

Andreas.

Sir Tiberius Ferretus III squeaked and curled tighter into Medusa's cloak. His silence was respectful now. Even he seemed to sense the weight of the moment.

"Then he's the reason you followed her through the Mirror?" Hades asked.

Medusa nodded. "Yes. And she knew it. She used the crossing to erase the memory. But not the drive."

"That's why the realm welcomed you like a queen," Loki said. "It wasn't a throne, it was a distraction."

"She gave me a crown," Medusa said, her voice low. "So, I'd forget the man I once loved enough to cross realms for."

Far away, in a chamber woven from fractured glass and stolen dreams, Arexia stirred.

She stood before a burning pool of reflections, staring at herself in a dozen variations, each twisted slightly differently.

But none of them smiled.

She turned.

The Mirror Maze shimmered around her. Offbeat. Rebellious. Wrong.

Something was missing.
Something was out of her control.

A flicker. A name.
Andreas.

She snarled.

"They remember."

She hissed a single command into the air:

"Burn the Whisper Vault."

Back in the maze, Medusa dropped the map.

Her breath caught.

"The Vault," she said. "She's going to destroy it."

"How do you know?" Zeus asked.

"I felt it."

"No more waiting," she said, standing. "We move now. Through the Grove of Unspoken Names. Around the Dead Echoes. Straight into the Whisper Vault."

"And if she finds us first?" Hades asked.

Medusa didn't hesitate.

"Then we remind her why I followed her through that Mirror in the first place."

Her fingers clenched the map tighter.

"She took him from me twice," she whispered. "Athena gave me a version of Andreas that wasn't mine. I convinced myself I imagined the difference. That maybe war changed him. But it didn't."

Her voice broke into a growl. "Because he wasn't him."

Loki's eyes widened.

"The real Andreas …" he said slowly, "was never returned."

"No," Medusa said. "She buried him here. In this realm. In the one place none of us would think to look."

"The Vault," Hades breathed.

"Then let's go crack it open," Ares said, his sword already flaming.

The flames flared blue.

The map pulsed.

And the shadows whispered the name of the one who'd been taken… and the goddess who was done letting anyone rewrite her truth.

Chapter 35: The Grove of Unspoken Names

They entered at dusk.

Or at least, it felt like dusk.

In the Realm of Echoes, time bent around emotion and this place? It felt like grief was sinking into the soil.

No trees here grew the same way twice. Their trunks twisted in agony or curled inward like secrets trying not to be spoken. The leaves didn't rustle. They murmured. Hissed. Muttered names like curses carried on the wind.

Ares lifted his sword. "I don't like this."

"Good," Loki whispered. "That means it's working."

They followed the map in silence.

Sir Tiberius Ferretus III led the way now, bounding ahead through the underbrush like he'd once owned the place. His little monocle glinted with every flick of moonlight.

Then the whispers began.

"Unworthy."
"Forgotten."
"Too late."

"They're just echoes," Hades muttered. "Don't listen."

But they did listen.

Because suddenly, the voices knew things.

"Why didn't you save him the first time?"

Medusa flinched.

No one had spoken.

The voice had come from beneath her feet, curling up through the roots.

"You knew he wasn't the same," the voice continued. "You kissed him anyway. You buried the doubt. You crowned the lie."

"Stop," Medusa growled.

The wind didn't stop.

It carried another whisper.

"You forgot his laugh."

She staggered.

"I didn't," she hissed.

But she had. She couldn't remember it now. Just the silence he'd left behind.

Persephone gasped and stumbled against a tree. Its bark shimmered with her old self, the girl with flowers in her hair and blood on her hands.

"Don't stop walking," Hades said. "If we linger, it'll pull us under."

"What is this place?" Hera asked.

"The Grove of Unspoken Names," Loki said. "It was designed to hold the memories gods wanted to forget. And the truths mortals couldn't survive."

"Perfect vacation spot," Hercules muttered, shielding his face from a branch that whispered his mother's disappointment.

The grove opened ahead of them.

A circle of trees loomed twisted and blackened, their bark branded with names in a thousand languages. Some glowed. Some bled.

One of them burned faintly with letters Medusa recognised.

ANDREAS.

She ran to it.

The tree pulsed at her touch.

The name writhed.

A voice, low, male, familiar, whispered from the trunk:

"You're close."

Her breath caught. "Andreas?"

But the tree darkened again.

And across the clearing... a glow pulsed.

A path revealed itself thorned, gold-veined, leading downward into the roots of the realm.

Toward the Whisper Vault.

Behind them, the grove trembled.

Arexia had found them.

And the grove began to scream.

Chapter 36: The Vault of Stolen Voices

The path opened like a wound in the earth.

Gold-veined roots clawed downward into the dark, each step echoing with the whisper of names too painful to remember. Not all of them belonged to gods.

Some were mortal.

Some were hers.

Medusa led them in silence.

Behind her, Hades summoned a dim flame to light the descent. Loki whistled softly, the tune echoing back wrong. Ares walked with his blade drawn. Hera gripped Persephone's hand.

And Sir Tiberius Ferretus III sat firmly on Medusa's shoulder, alert, still, as if he too knew this place was sacred.

Not holy.

Buried.

They reached the bottom in a hush that didn't feel like silence.

It felt like something was listening.

The Vault of Stolen Voices wasn't a door. It was a wall of stone that pulsed like a throat. Etched across its surface were the unspoken, carved in spectral script that flickered and wept.

There were no locks.

Only a command:

"Speak what was silenced."

Loki arched a brow. "If this is another riddle, I'm skipping straight to arson."

"It's not a riddle," Medusa said quietly.

She stepped forward.

"I loved him," she said.

The stone pulsed once.

"I loved Andreas before the gods ever feared me. Before the throne. Before the curse. Before the crown of serpents."

The others stood still.

"I loved him when I was still soft. And when he was taken, I became sharp."

The Vault groaned.

"But I knew," she said, breath hitching. "I knew the Andreas Athena gave back wasn't mine. His eyes were empty. His voice was quiet. I told myself I was imagining it. That I was broken. That war had changed us both."

She stepped closer.

"But the truth was stolen from me."

She laid her hand against the stone.

"I want it back."

The Vault split with a gasp.

Air hissed from within, cold, metallic, and furious.

And inside?

Not gold.

Not treasure.

Not even bones.

Just voices.

Hundreds. Thousands. Suspended like constellations in a vast chamber of mist and memory. They moved like stars whispering, weeping, screaming, singing.

And in the centre...

A single orb of shadow.

Loki stepped forward. "That's it, isn't it?"

Medusa nodded.

Her voice cracked. "That's him."

But the shadows stirred.

And the orb shuddered.

From the mist, a figure stepped forward cloaked in silver flame, eyes like razors.

Arexia.

She smiled.

“Ah,” she said. “So, you found him.”

Her gaze turned to the orb.

“What a shame. He was safer when he was silent.”

Medusa’s voice dropped to a growl.

“So were you.”

Chapter 37: The Voice That Broke the Silence

The Vault shook.

Not violently.

Not with rage.

It trembled the way a heartbeat does when it's forgotten how to feel.

Arexia stepped closer to the shadow-orb, her silver cloak trailing ash behind her. "Do you know what he asked for when I took him?" she said softly. "You."

She smiled.

"And then he screamed."

Medusa stepped in front of the orb, shielding it with her body. "Say his name again. I dare you."

Arexia's grin sharpened. "Andreas."

The orb pulsed.

A low vibration filled the chamber, like sound dragging itself out of death.

The mist swirled faster. The voices quieted. And then for the first time in what felt like lifetimes, a single, fragile word echoed in the dark:

"Medusa."

Her knees almost buckled.

"Andreas?" she whispered, turning to the orb. "Is it really?"

"You remembered me."

It wasn't a question.

It was a lifeline.

Loki stood frozen. Even Ares lowered his sword.

From within the orb, light began to break through, not golden, not divine. Human. Raw. Real. A warmth Medusa hadn't felt since before she was remade.

"You're real," she breathed. "They took you, and they gave me back a ghost."

"And you kissed the ghost," Andreas's voice rasped. "Because you didn't know."

"I know now."

Arexia hissed. "He belongs to the Vault. His voice is stolen property."

Medusa turned slowly, serpents rising.

"He's not property. He's mine."

"You'll destroy him," Arexia snapped. "He was meant to be silent! A memory! A warning!"

"Then let me be the lesson."

Medusa struck her hand into the orb, and it shattered.

Light exploded outward.

The Vault screamed.

The chamber cracked at its roots as a figure collapsed into Medusa's arms, flesh and breath and shaking limbs and eyes wide with wonder.

Andreas.

His voice was hoarse, but whole.

"I told you, "He whispered. "You'd come."

Arexia screamed, drawing on the realm itself, mirrors breaking, walls unravelling, all of Echoes beginning to spiral.

But Medusa stood tall.

Serpents flaring. Eyes blazing. Andreas behind her, voice unbound.

And she said the words that cracked the realm in two:

"You don't own my story anymore."

Chapter 38: The Realm Breaks Open

The scream wasn't human.

It wasn't divine.

It was Realm-deep the sound of a reality tearing at the seams.

Arexia's power lashed out like wildfire, her silver flame turning black at the edges. The Vault cracked behind her, shattered voices spilling upward like ghosts clawing their way free.

Andreas clung to Medusa, breath shallow, eyes locked on the goddess who had stolen his name.

"You shouldn't have done that," Arexia snarled.

Medusa didn't flinch. "You shouldn't have taken him."

"You think this is a rescue?" Arexia raised both arms. The realm groaned. Mirrors burst. Walls bled memory. "You just tore open the fabric of Echoes!"

"I did what you were afraid to do," Medusa said. "I listened."

The ground split beneath them.

From the cracks poured scenes from the past, fractured, frantic, and half-formed. Not illusions. Not memories. Truths.

Andreas's abduction.
Athena's bargain.
Arexia whispering lies into a mirror too powerful to break.

The others staggered back, shielding themselves from the flood of raw, bleeding story.

Loki caught one with his bare hands, a memory shaped like a blade.

He hissed. "She rewrote everything."

Zeus blinked as an entire alternate version of himself flickered past, crownless, forgotten, weak. "Is that... me?!"

Hades cursed as a vision of Persephone chained to a throne she never claimed slid across the floor like spilled ink.

The realm wasn't just collapsing.

It was correcting.

"We need to leave," Hera said, steadying herself.

"No," Medusa said, stepping forward. "We end this."

Ares stood beside her. "Together?"

Medusa nodded.

With Andreas behind her, Loki to her right, and her army of misfit gods around her, she raised her voice.

"You wanted to control the story, Arexia," she said. "But here's the truth"

She placed her hand over her heart.

"I remember now."

The light from the Vault surged upward.

A column of power tore through the ceiling, punching into the sky of the Realms and shattering it.

Stars blinked out.

Clouds unravelled into sentences half-written.

And far above them, the Tree of Realms groaned as its roots bent to watch.

Arexia stumbled, hands burning. Her flame sputtered. Her reflection fractured.

"You don't understand what you've done," she whispered. "The Realms weren't ready"

"They never are," Medusa said.

And the ground caved in.

They fell together.

Not into darkness.

Into truth.

Chapter 39: The Realms Remember

They didn't hit the ground.

They became it.

Each of them scattered across different points in the shattered realm flung like pages torn from a book and dropped out of order.

Medusa blinked against a sky she didn't recognise.

No sun. No stars.
Just threads of story unravelling in midair, glowing sentences curling through space like constellations trying to rewrite themselves.

She sat up.

"Andreas?"

No answer.

She was alone.

Across the fractured realm…

Hades stood ankle-deep in a swamp of memories, watching shadows rise like smoke from the water.

Loki woke inside a library built of glass. Every book whispered names he wasn't supposed to know.

Hera paced a courtroom with no walls, listening to echoes argue her regrets.

Ares was already fighting a memory that bled.

Persephone wandered through a garden where every flower bloomed into something she once buried.

Zeus found a mirror that didn't reflect him at all.

And Andreas?

Andreas knelt before a statue that looked like Medusa... but younger.

Unguarded.
Unbroken.
Human.

He touched the stone cheek gently.

"You remember," he whispered, voice hoarse. "So now... do I?"

The statue cracked.

Somewhere, above and beneath it all, the Tree of Realms groaned louder.

Its roots coiled through the broken sky, drinking in every truth that had been forgotten, rewritten, or stolen.

It remembered.

It remembered all of it.

The lies.
The edits.
The sacrifices.
The names.

And as each piece of the realm awakened voices, lands, gods, and mortals, it didn't break apart.

It started to bloom.

Medusa stood at the edge of a hill made of story.

The air shimmered with old words made new.

In the distance, she could see the threads glowing lines of memory reaching toward one another like vines.

Her vines.

Her truth.

And Andreas, a dot of light moving toward her.

The Realms hadn't collapsed.

They had been waiting.

Waiting for someone to remember.

Chapter 40: The Story Rewrites Itself

The threads of the Realms shimmered around her.

Some tangled.
Some frayed.
Some waited.

Medusa stood in the centre of it all, the rewritten and the forgotten swirling at her feet like ribbons of light. The Tree of Realms above her glowed with silent expectation, its roots humming with memory.

And in her hands?

A quill.

Simple. Black. Made from a feather she hadn't realised she carried all this time.

It pulsed.

Alive.

"The Realm is waiting," came a voice behind her.

Andreas.

He stepped forward slowly, no longer the fractured echo she once kissed in a lie. His voice was steady now. Real.

She didn't turn to him yet.

"I don't want to rewrite everything," she said.

"You don't have to."

She turned then.

Andreas's eyes held hers. "But you can rewrite your place in it."

Loki appeared next, dusted in ink and smirking like he'd just survived a novella.

"I recommend lots of footnotes," he said. "And at least one chapter where I win."

Hades appeared beside him. "Or we burn the book."

Persephone smiled. "Or plant it."

Hera simply said, "Choose."

Ares cracked his knuckles. "Or punch it into a poem."

Zeus muttered, "Just don't make me a footnote again."

The quill grew warmer in her hand.

The Realms whispered to her.

They didn't want a perfect queen.

Or a monstrous icon.

Or a goddess tamed.

They wanted her.

The one who remembered.

The one who refused to be edited.

Medusa stepped forward and raised the quill.

The sky split not in chaos, but in invitation.

She wrote one line.

Not a prophecy.

Not a spell.

Just truth.

"I am not what they made me. I am what I remember."

The quill dissolved.

The light spread.

And across the Realms, memory and magic bloomed wild, tangled, imperfect...

True.

Chapter 41: The Root and the Rewrite

The Realms held their breath.

Above, the stars stilled.
Below, the earth pulsed like a heartbeat under the soil.

And in the centre of it all, the Tree of Realms moved.

Not with wind.
Not with magic.

With intention.

Its roots, thick, silver-veined, older than memory, rose from the ground and spiralled around Medusa's feet.

One coiled gently around her wrist.
Another brushed the side of Andreas's cheek
like a parent recognizing a child too long lost.

Then came the voice.

It didn't speak aloud.

It entered her.

"You remembered yourself.
But not all of us have.
Would you like to see what the first seed
remembers?"

Medusa nodded.

The Realms peeled open.

She didn't move but the world folded around
her like a book opening in reverse. Time
unspooled. Stars rewound. Words flowed
backward into ink.

She saw...

- A flame-lit grove before gods had names.
- The first mirror not glass, but still water kissed by lightning.
- The first rewrite, when truth was edited for the comfort of power.

And then she saw Arexia.

Younger. Smaller. Alone.

Carving her name into the bark of the Tree, whispering:

"I'll make them remember me."

But she hadn't waited for memory.

She had forced it.

The vision vanished.

Medusa stood again at the base of the Tree.

Andreas beside her.

The gods at her back.

And the Tree's voice, one last time:

"A name carved in truth needs no crown to last."

Medusa stepped forward and reached into the bark.

She didn't carve her name.

She planted it.

A single drop of ink.
A curl of story.
A memory returned without needing to be rewritten.

And the Tree bloomed again not with flowers.

With faces.

People forgotten.

Truths erased.

Songs never finished.

The Realms didn't just remember now.

They grew from it.

Chapter 42: The Crown She Never Asked For

The tree stopped blooming.

Not in death.

In reverence.

Every face it had grown turned toward Medusa expressions open, expectant, waiting.

A breeze passed through the Realms. It didn't rustle the leaves.

It bowed.

And in the hush that followed, a crown formed.

It didn't fall from the sky.
It didn't rise from a throne.

It grew slowly from the highest branch of the Tree, woven of bark, memory, ink, and names.

No gold. No jewels.

Just truth.

And it hovered above her head.

Waiting.

Medusa didn't move.

The others stood back, watching her. No one
spoke.

Even Loki, for once, said nothing.
Even Andreas didn't reach for her hand.

Because they all knew

This crown wasn't made to be worn.

It was made to test her.

Her fingers twitched. She could feel it above her humming with power, heavy with story.

She thought of:

- The first time she was rewritten.
- The ghost of Andreas returned in chains.
- The serpents she'd once called monsters.
- The gods who feared her.
- The girl who cried in front of a mirror and didn't recognize her face.

She stepped forward.

She could wear it.

She could become it.

But instead...

She bowed.

The crown drifted down, touched her hair

And shattered into seeds.

They scattered into the wind.

Some landed in soil.

Some found mirrors.

Some flew so far, they crossed Realms.

And all of them carried one truth:

Power isn't proven by who wears the crown.

It's revealed by who remembers they never

needed one.

Andreas stepped beside her.

"Now what?" he asked.

Medusa smiled faintly.

"We tell the story right this time."

Chapter 43: The Library of Threads

It wasn't a throne room.

It wasn't a battlefield.

It was a library.

But not like any Medusa had ever seen.

The shelves were alive vines of ink curling upward into the sky, looping through scrolls that whispered as they unrolled themselves. Each page pulsed with light. Some glowed softly. Some flickered like forgotten fireflies. Some wept.

These were not books.

They were lives.

Unwritten.

Half-written.

Erased.

Waiting.

Andreas stood at her side, one hand resting lightly on her back.

Loki had already scaled one of the taller scroll towers and was upside down, reading something aloud to a cluster of talking quills.

"I think this one ends with a cursed pie," he said. "Delightful. Absolutely publishable."

A tiny voice squeaked from the nearest scroll: "That was my grandmother."

"My condolences," Loki said cheerfully.

Medusa stepped into the centre of the archive. The ink beneath her feet rearranged itself to form a path. With each step, forgotten stories rose and unspooled around her like silk ribbons coming home.

There was no crown on her head.

But the shelves bowed anyway.

The Realms remembered her now.

Not as a villain.

Not as a queen.

Not as a cautionary tale.

As a thread-keeper.

Andreas picked up a blank scroll. "How do we start?"

Medusa smiled, took his hand, and dipped a quill into ink made from the first mirror's light.

"We don't start," she said. "We continue."

She wrote:

"Once upon a time, a story remembered its storyteller."

And with that, the Realms began to write themselves again.

Chapter 44: The Feather That Remained

Long after the others had drifted into quiet laughter,

after Loki's enchanted quills had started a rebellion in the poetry section,

after Andreas had fallen asleep beside an unfinished tale, he was sure he knew the ending to

Medusa sat alone.

The Library of Threads hummed around her.

Not loud.

Not urgent.

Just aware.

A faint pulse in the ink. A breath between pages.

And something... waiting.

She almost didn't notice it.

A single feather.

Black. Soft. Threaded with glints of silver and gold.

It wasn't one she had used to write.

It hadn't been dipped in ink.
It hadn't fallen from a scroll.
It had been left.

On the floor beside her. Silent.

And tucked beneath it a note, written in a hand she hadn't seen in a long time:

"You remembered yourself.
But do you remember me?"

- A.

Medusa didn't move.

Not right away.

Because she recognized the script.

Not from this realm.

Not even from Olympus.

From a mirror.

From before.

Arexia.

But not the one who had stolen Andreas.

Not the one who fractured the realms.

This was... earlier.

A version of her that hadn't yet turned power into fear.

A girl who had once stood beside Medusa and whispered:

"If they won't give us a crown, let's make our own."

The feather pulsed.

And just for a moment brief as a blink Medusa felt something stir beneath the library itself.

Not memory.
Not story.
A presence.

Something left behind.

Something unfinished.

And then it vanished.

Medusa stared at the feather in her hand.

She didn't say a word.

But the Library heard her thought anyway.

"There's one more story, isn't there?"

And far below her, in the root-ink depths beneath the Realms…

A mirror cracked.

Chapter 45: The Forgotten Rewrite

The mirror cracked...

And the Realms did not break.

They breathed.

As if some ancient truth had finally exhaled after holding its breath for centuries.

Medusa followed the pulse.

The feather trembled in her hand, leading her not through a doorway, but down a spiral of ink that formed beneath her feet. The library unfolded, spiralled, then folded in again an origami memory reshaping itself for her eyes alone.

Not even Loki could see where she was going.

Not even Andreas could follow.

This was hers.

And hers alone.

She stepped into a chamber lit by starlight but not from the sky.

The stars were written.
Script curled in constellations.
Memory stitched into the ceiling.

And at the centre...

A mirror.

Small.

Dusty.

Fractured.

Just like the one she had first seen herself in

not as a monster, not as a goddess, but as a girl

asking:

"What if I'm more than what they fear?"

Someone stood in front of it.

Back turned.
Hair in tight coils.
Cloak stitched with thorns and lullabies.

She turned.

And Medusa's breath caught.

It was Arexia.

But not the one who stole the Realms.

This was... before.

Younger. Sadder. Kinder.

Her eyes were storm clouds hiding poems.

And in her hand?

A scroll Medusa recognized.

Her own story.

"You left," Medusa whispered.

Arexia nodded. "You forgot."

They stood in silence.

No magic. No music. No gods watching.

Just two girls who once dreamed of building a crown out of story.

Arexia offered the scroll.

"You wrote it wrong," she said.

Medusa took it gently. "Then help me write it right."

Behind them, the stars shifted.
The Realms leaned closer.

And in a voice made of roots and echoes, they whispered:

"Let the truth be told."

Chapter 46: The Rewrite Begins

The scroll hovered between them.

Not heavy, not fragile, just... waiting.

Arexia placed a hand beside Medusa's, and for the first time in a thousand mirrored realities, they wrote together.

Ink bled gold.

Words didn't form in lines.
They formed in threads dancing across the parchment like silk spun from truths too long silenced.

Medusa wrote the first name.

Arexia wrote the second.

Not the names they were given.

But the names they chose.

One by one, the Realms began to pulse.

Far above, in the library, the shelves shivered.

Andreas woke with a jolt, looking toward the spiral path that no longer existed.

Loki narrowed his eyes at the quills trying to unionize the ink pot.
"Something's shifting," he murmured.
"Something... old."

Back in the chamber of stars, the story began to change.

Not erasure.

Reclamation.

The war was not erased but retold with truth.

The villains were not vanished but faced.

The pain was not hidden but honoured.

And the girls who had once been forgotten?

They stood in the centre of the rewrite not as symbols.

As authors.

Arexia glanced up, her voice raw. "Do you think they'll let us finish it?"

Medusa smiled.

"They'll try to stop us."

She dipped the quill again.

"Let them try."

And with that, the story shifted again not forward, not back, but inward curling into every Realm, every root, every reader.

Not a new beginning.

But a rightful return.

Chapter 47: The Realm That Never Was

It began with a name.

Not one spoken.

Not one written.

One that had been erased.

And as Medusa's quill danced across the page with Arexia's beside hers, the Library of Threads shuddered.

Somewhere between root and realm, a shelf collapsed.

Scrolls fell like dying stars.

And a single book bound in black glass, chained in rusted gold, opened.

Above, Andreas felt it first.

He dropped the scroll he'd been reading, his breath catching.

"What was that?"

Loki tilted his head. "A forgotten story... clawing its way out."

Hercules blinked. "That sounds... normal for this group."

"No," Loki said. "This one doesn't want to be remembered. It wants to be real."

Back beneath the stars, the chamber cracked.

The mirror behind Medusa and Arexia flickered, then split in half.

And through the jagged glass, a Realm bled into view.

Not Olympus.

Not any of the Ten.

A Realm no one remembered because it had been cut from the story entirely.

Its skies were stitched from ink.
Its rivers ran backward.
Its trees whispered warnings in languages that hadn't been spoken since the first myth was told.

"Where is that?" Medusa asked.

Arexia's hand trembled.
"That's the Realm I was made in. Not born made."

Medusa turned slowly. "You're saying…?"

Arexia nodded, pain blooming in her eyes.

"I wasn't supposed to be part of the Realms at all.

I was the rewrite they locked away."

And from the shadows of the broken mirror...
Something watched.

Not a god.
Not a monster.

A girl.

A girl with Arexia's face but younger.
Sharper.
Wrong.

She smiled.

And the mirror whispered:

"The Forgotten Realm remembers you."

Chapter 48: The Girl Who Wasn't Chosen

She stepped through the mirror with no sound.

No crack of magic.

No chorus of prophecy.

Just the soft pat of bare feet on starlit stone.

She looked like Arexia.

She moved like her.

But when Medusa looked into her eyes…

There was no soul behind them.

Only calculation.

"Who are you?" Medusa asked, her voice firm.

The girl tilted her head. "That depends. Who am I allowed to be today?"

Arexia stepped back, her voice shaking. "She's the fragment. The piece they cut from me and left to rot in the Realm That Never Was."

The girl curtsied.

"They called me an error.
But I kept the best parts."

Her presence warped the chamber.

Ink bled upward from the cracks.
The constellations above blinked out one by one.
The scroll in Medusa's hand shook violently, its threads unravelling as if this girl's very existence undid meaning.

"You can't be here," Arexia whispered.

The girl grinned. "I already am."

Then she looked at Medusa. Really looked.

"You want to fix the story," she said. "But what if it was never broken?"

Medusa didn't flinch. "It was built on silencing us."

"And rewriting it?" The girl raised an eyebrow. "You'll only become the next silencer."

Arexia stepped between them. "Leave her alone."

The girl's expression darkened.

"No," she said. "I've been left alone long enough."

She held out her hand, and from the void behind her, a mirror-quill formed.
Its ink shimmered in void-light.
It didn't write truth. It wrote undoing.

"I'm not here to change the story," she whispered.

"I'm here to erase all of you from it."

And then she wrote.

One word.

And the chamber cracked open.

Chapter 49: The Ink That Burned the Realms

The word she wrote was short. Sharp.

And final.

It didn't translate.
It didn't echo.

It devoured.

The scroll in Medusa's hands burst into flame,
not fire, but ink-fire.
Black and glimmering, like constellations
choking on themselves.

The stars above screamed.

The floor split in half.

And from the centre of the chamber, a crack
raced toward the roots of the Realms.

Arexia collapsed.

Medusa tried to run to her, but her legs refused to move.

The mirror-quill girl tilted her head.

"I didn't unmake you," she said. "Yet."

Medusa's rage flared.

"You think this makes you powerful?"

"No," the girl said. "This makes me free."

Above, in the Realm Library, Andreas fell to one knee.

Loki caught him just before he hit the floor.

"Hey. No dying. That's not in your contract."

Andreas gritted his teeth.

"She wrote something. Not a rewrite. A correction."

Loki stiffened.

"Oh no. Not a correction. That's worse than a plot twist."

Hercules and Ares sprinted down the nearest staircase.
Ink smoke began bleeding from the scrolls, choking the air with unwritten truths.

Ares drew his blade. "We fight whatever comes through that mirror."

"And if it's not a monster?" Hercules asked.

Ares didn't blink. "Then we stab it more carefully."

Back below, Medusa grabbed Arexia's hand.

"Don't let go," she whispered.

Arexia's eyes fluttered. "She's not just a fragment. She's the piece that remembers what we were before the gods."

Medusa's blood ran cold.

Because now... she remembered too.

Before the crowns.
Before the stories.
There was only the scream.
The first girl who said no.

And that girl had written again.

Chapter 50: The First Rewrite

The Realms didn't break.

They remembered.

The moment the girl's correction spilled across the floor, everything shivered. Not shattered. Not crumbled.
Just shifted.

Like a dream, remembering what it was before it became a nightmare.

In the Realm Library, scrolls began writing themselves backward.

Names that had been erased bled through in violet ink.
Mothers. Daughters. Queens.

Some names had no realm of origin.

Because they were from the before-before.

The stories that were buried before the gods arrived.

Andreas stared in horror. "This isn't a rewrite... It's a return."

Below, Medusa and Arexia clung to each other as the chamber pulsed.

The mirror-quill girl floated now, her feet no longer touching the ground. Her eyes were white with starlight.

"Once," she said, "the story belonged to us."

"And then?" Medusa asked, jaw clenched.

"It was taken."

Golden vines curled through the chamber, winding around Arexia's feet.

She gasped. "These were mine. From my beginning."

Medusa nodded slowly. "Then maybe... It's time we stop rewriting what they gave us."

"And start remembering what we wrote first."

The mirror cracked again.

And this time, it showed a Realm that hadn't been seen since the stars were young.

No crowns.
No thrones.
Just girls with ink-stained hands and mouths full of fire.

The First Rewrite.

And it had just begun.

Chapter 51: The Mouths That Spoke Fire

They weren't warriors.

They weren't queens.

They were the first storytellers.

And they had teeth.

The mirror flared open, not broken, not

bleeding.

Burning.

Through it stepped the First Circle.

Not goddesses.

Not mortals.

But something older. Wilder. Forgotten.

Girls with flame around their wrists and ink on

their tongues.

They didn't walk. They declared themselves into the chamber.

Arexia gasped. "I've seen them before. In the scrolls we were never meant to read."

Medusa whispered, "They're real?"

One of the First Circle turned, fire trailing from her breath.
"Oh, darling," she said with a wicked grin, "we've been waiting."

The mirror-quill girl faltered.

These weren't her allies.
They weren't here to erase.

They were here to reignite.

"You used the wrong word," one of them said to her.

"It was the only word I had left," the girl replied.

"Then let us teach you more."

They gathered around Medusa and Arexia not as enemies, but as mentors.

"We don't rewrite the world with silence," one said.
"We do it with story."

"And story," another added, "must always burn a little."

Medusa stepped forward, voice shaking but clear.

"Then show us how."

And the First Circle smiled.

Not kindly.

But like fire meeting dry forest.

The kind of smile that promised:
This time, no one forgets us again.

Chapter 52: The Flame and the Quill

The First Circle didn't explain.

They demonstrated.

One girl stepped forward, her eyes lit from within by starlit embers.
She dipped her fingers in ink not from a well, but her veins.

With a single stroke, she painted a symbol into the air.

It hovered.

It sang.

And then it exploded into flame and became a door.

Medusa took a step back. "You wrote fire?"

The girl shrugged.
"We wrote consequence. Fire just likes to come along for the ride."

The mirror-quill girl, still kneeling, looked up.
"You knew the cost. You lit the story anyway."

Another of the First Circle laughed.
"Of course. Power without story is just control. And we weren't made to be quiet."

Arexia reached for Medusa's hand. "Do you feel that?"

Medusa nodded slowly.

It wasn't magic.

It wasn't prophecy.

It was the thrum of the original narrative waking up.

Something older than the gods.
Older than time.

Truth, unfiltered and wild.

Loki, standing far above in the observation hall, pressed his face to the glass.

He grinned.
"Oh, good. The plot is on fire again."

Ares groaned.
"We just fixed the library."

As the flames shaped new stories into the air, the First Circle turned to Medusa.

"It's your turn," one said. "Tell the truth the gods feared most."

Medusa blinked. "Which one?"

The First Circle smiled.

"The one you never said out loud."

Chapter 53: The Rewrite She Didn't See Coming

The First Circle had lit the fire.

The quill had burned.

The truth had been spoken.

And for a heartbeat, everything felt... still.

Medusa stood at the centre of the blaze, her voice trembling, but proud. "I am not the villain of your stories. I am the fire you tried to bury."

Arexia's eyes shimmered not with defiance, but with something gentler.
Grief.

"I believe you," she whispered.

Then she turned.

And reached into the flame.

"No!" Medusa grabbed her wrist. "You can't"

"It's the only way to stop them from erasing you again," Arexia said softly. "If I rewrite the Realms before they can, I can make it safe. A realm where no one needs to remember... because nothing ever went wrong."

Medusa's serpents hissed. "You don't know what that will cost."

Arexia looked at her, eyes wide with sorrow. "Yes, I do."

She released Medusa's hand.

And wrote.

One word.

A name.

Medusa.

The world shook.

Not violently.

Quietly.

Like breath being held.

The mirrors bent light into ribbon. The First Circle vanished in flame. The gods froze mid-step.

And Medusa fell.

She hit marble.

Polished. Untouched.
Perfect.

A temple stretched around her, unfamiliar but soothing.
She sat up slowly, eyes narrowing.

No mirrors.

No flames.

No serpents.

Just a sky painted in lavender and birds that chirped in harmony.

Steps echoed behind her.

She turned.

Andreas stood at the top of the stairs. Smiling.

Holding Arexia's hand.

They were dressed in white. Regal. Calm.

Married?

Medusa rose to her feet. "Andreas?"

He tilted his head.
"I'm sorry... do I know you?"

Ares strode past her, chatting with Hercules. Hades gave a rare laugh. Hera watered a blooming garden. Persephone taught children to dance.

Peace.

Everywhere.

She ran.

From one building to the next.

No statues bore her face.
No scrolls carried her name.

No one looked twice.

Medusa didn't exist.

And from somewhere unseen, a whisper.

Arexia's voice.

"Welcome to the world you never ruined."

Then... silence.

And a mirror that refused to open.

About the Author

Holly Symons accidentally created a multiverse and hasn't stopped writing since. A lifelong lover of mythology, fantasy, and stories where chaos wears a crown, Holly weaves epic adventures full of flawed immortals, forgotten realms, and heroines who rewrite destiny (and occasionally the rules of space-time).

When she's not chasing dragons through tangled timelines or wrangling a goat named Buttermunch, she's dreaming up worlds that blend humour, heart, and high-stakes magic. The RealmsVerse of Mirrors: The Realm That Forgot Her is one of many stories in Holly's ever-expanding universe where laughter and longing go hand-in-hand and no prophecy is safe from a twist.

She lives in Australia and writes with a cup of bubble tea, a stack of notebooks, and a fierce determination to bring mythic chaos to your bookshelf.